OLD SOLDIERS

Paul Bailey, who was a Literary Fellow at the Universities of Newcastle and Durham, was the first recipient of the E. M. Forster Award. For *At the Jerusalem* he won a Somerset Maugham Award and an Arts Council Award for the best first novel published between 1963 and 1967. In 1976 a bicentennial fellowship took him to the midwest of America. In 1979 he was honoured with a George Orwell Memorial Prize for his essay 'The Limitations of Despair' published in the *Listener*. His other novels include *Trespasses*, *A Distant Likeness* and *Peter Smart's Confessions*.

PAUL BAILEY

OLD SOLDIERS

for Pam –
gratefully –

Paul Bailey

A KING PENGUIN
PUBLISHED BY PENGUIN BOOKS

Penguin Books Ltd, 27 Wrights Lane, London w8 5tz (Publishing and Editorial)
and Harmondsworth, Middlesex, England (Distribution and Warehouse)
Viking Penguin Inc., 40 West 23rd Street, New York, New York 10010, USA
Penguin Books Australia Ltd, Ringwood, Victoria, Australia
Penguin Books Canada Ltd, 2801 John Street, Markham, Ontario, Canada l3r 1b4
Penguin Books (NZ) Ltd, 182–190 Wairau Road, Auckland 10, New Zealand

First published by Jonathan Cape 1980
Published in Penguin Books 1982
Reprinted 1987

Copyright © Paul Bailey, 1980
All rights reserved

Made and printed in Great Britain by
Richard Clay Ltd, Bungay, Suffolk
Set in Caslon

'Lurks a god's laughter
In this?' he said,
'That I am the living
And she the dead!'

> THOMAS HARDY: 'After the War'

Pistol speaks naught but truth.

> SHAKESPEARE: *Henry IV, Part Two*

For
David Healy

One

Too sick with grief for tears, Victor Harker arrived in London smiling. People smiled back at him as he willed his body out of King's Cross Station. He was unaware of them, seeing only his dead wife, Stella.

When he reached the street, she left him. His luggage, weightless before, suddenly became heavy. He stopped. For several minutes, he stood still in the city he had vowed long ago he would never return to. Then a taxi driver, acknowledging his smile with a nod, relieved him of his suitcases.

In the cab, he closed his eyes. London had been his prison once. He had made his vow on the nineteenth of September, 1922, at noon precisely — he had made it, and fled. The train taking him to the north had moved at a sluggish pace, he remembered — there had been many stops on the journey. During one of them, beyond York, he had stared at an embankment covered with ragwort for nearly an hour. The sight of a hare scuttling across it had caused his heart to leap — he'd known, instantly, that he too had somewhere to go. He had never eaten hare — whether jugged or roasted — by way of thanks for what the animal had told him.

The bright future it had signalled was his bright past now. 'Stella,' he whispered.

In the hotel room, he heard his father's whine. Earth had failed to smother that hated snivelling – it burst upon Victor Harker now, with all its old power to enrage. It told of Billy Harker's misery; of Billy Harker's weakness; of Billy Harker's longing to cease being Billy Harker : 'I can't abide this life of mine no more, Vic. I want to be done with it.'

The words stopped, and were replaced by a howl that had brought Billy's son out of sleep a thousand times, if not more, in the fifty-four years since Billy's death.

'You can stay in my dreams. I don't want you plaguing me while I'm awake.'

There were no voices to disturb him as he un-packed. He put away his neatly folded shirts; hung up his carefully pressed suits and trousers. When everything was in its proper place, he switched on the television. The sound of people screaming preceded the picture – a smoke-filled Belfast street, and what remained of an insurance building. A man had been blinded; another had lost his legs; a woman was in the rubble.

He gave himself a reproving lecture while he ran a bath. The loss of Stella was as nothing compared to what the majority of humankind were enduring at this very moment. 'Nothing,' he said, testing the water. 'Nothing.' And yet his heart ached.

He dried himself thoroughly and then dressed for dinner. He would eat moderately, as was his custom : a chop, perhaps, or a fillet of sole. He would indulge in a little wine.

'No, nothing,' he told his gloomy reflection.

Appearances were deceptive, but they mattered.

It was time to put on a show again. He adjusted an idiot's grin into a look of contentment, said 'Nothing' once more, and made his way to the dining-room.

His first night in London passed slowly. Hour after hour, the blessings he most craved — death, or its substitute, a dreamless sleep — eluded him. In old age, it seemed, he had at last become the son of his father. Now he, too, was seeking oblivion.

'But not with drink.'

Nor, he reminded himself, with pills. His pride had not deserted him : he had fought long and hard for the right to it ; he would not resort to a coward's methods.

'No.'

He hugged a pillow until daybreak, pressing it to him as if it were living flesh. He sometimes called it Stella.

The hands he saw were clawing air, were clutching at nothing. Wedding rings — gold for the officers ; brass for the ordinary seamen — glinted briefly on the water. A hundred sailors' wives would soon be widows.

After his vision, he returned to the bare facts, carved on a marble monument : on the seventh of September, 1870 — he read — Her Majesty's Ship *Captain* had foundered off Cape Finisterre. The sea had claimed the lives of all the men on board.

He mouthed the names of the dead : Ainsworth, J. ; Alebon, W. ; Austin, P. There followed a Baker, and a Barker ; a Barling, and a Beckett. Only their hands were real to him. They had no faces or voices.

He stopped at Blackler, T. — whoever he had been. He tried to give him blond hair and piggy eyes, and one of those chins that has a pronounced ridge down the middle, and the expected bow legs, and a tattoo on the right arm — but the separate parts wouldn't join. Tiring of the attempt, he walked towards the altar.

He looked up at the cathedral's dome. Some words from Psalms encircled it. How many of the *Captain*'s crew, he wondered, had praised Him in the sound of the trumpet, upon the lute and harp, in the cymbals and dance, upon the string and pipe?

Giddy from the effort of reading, he lowered his head. A tall, red-faced man was standing beside him, smiling.

'*Magnifique, n'est-ce-pas?*'

'*Je,*' Victor Harker said. '*Je suis un,*' he continued. 'I'm very sorry, but I don't speak French.'

'You don't? Are you telling me you're English?'

'Yes, I am.'

'Well, that's a nice surprise. Shake hands with me. It isn't every day one meets a fellow countryman in St Paul's. The name's Standish. Harold Standish. Captain Harold Standish.'

Victor Harker blinked the glinting rings away. 'Pleased to meet you, Captain. Harker.'

'Just Harker?'

'My friends call me Victor.'

'You've a strong English handshake, Victor Harker. Palm to palm, as it should be; nothing slippery about it. Military man, are you?'

'I fought in France. I left England as a private, and I came home as one.'

'It's the privates who win wars, Mr Harker. I was proud of the men I captained, and — in my less modest moments — I like to think that they were proud of me. They called me "Good old Captain Hal". I maintained discipline, of course — I was never one to countenance any larking about in the ranks — but I did it with courtesy; yes, courtesy. I assume you're religious?'

'No, I'm not.'

'Why are you here, then?'

'The history, I suppose.'

In the home that Billy Harker had failed to rule over there had been heat, not warmth. The coldness of churches had soothed Billy's angry son. He had found something like peace in their damp darkness.

'What is't o'clock?' Captain Standish winked. 'A historian as distinguished as yourself should know what I'm asking.'

'It's nearly twelve.'

'Time for a tipple, I should say. I wet my whistle at an ancient hostelry a stone's throw from here. You'll raise a glass with me?'

'Yes,' said Victor Harker. 'That would be pleasant.'

In a pub on Ludgate Hill, among his own respectable kind — bank employees, solicitors, clerks, lawyers — Victor Harker listened to his new acquaintance.

'Yes, my friend (you will pardon the familiarity, I feel certain), Captain Harold Standish is a guide these days. He shows people the sights. Historical monuments, and such. He does so with panache.

13

He does so with a little necessary invention. He has to. He needs to. How else would he survive?'

'How else?'

'How else? He doesn't know. The army was his life. His home was the mess. He's not happy in the civilian world. He finds it a dreadful place. He'd go off his rocker if he had to spend his time spewing up dry-as-dust facts about the illustrious dead. That's why he tarts things up a bit.'

'He doesn't — I mean, *you* don't tell the truth?'

'Here and there. On and off. You can't give Lord Nelson his eye and his arm back, can you? It depends on the tourists, and where they come from. Captain Hal has some rare old fun with Americans. You should have seen the prize specimen he chanced upon yesterday — a Mrs Ashmead Windle from California. He told her any amount of tommy-rot about Bishop Deorwulf.'

'Who?'

'You may well ask. Deorwulf was proclaimed Bishop of London in the year 860 : Anno Domini, it goes without saying. He comes between Ingwald and Smithwulf. The inquisitive Mrs Windle took a fancy to his name. Her obliging instructor spun a yarn and a half about Deorwulf's barely contained passion for a sprightly mother superior named Guinnefrede. Mrs W. was beguiled by their sorry tale : it had, to borrow a phrase the lady used, her heart in a flutter. It also put several pound notes in Captain Standish's wallet. You're a slow drinker.'

'I always have been.'

'There you're like Bishop Wine; or there again, perhaps you aren't. I'm in two minds where he's concerned. Sometimes I describe him as an old soak, kept upright by a couple of strong-armed choristers ; on other occasions I depict him as a model of temperance, a man inspired to sobriety by his very name. It depends, as I said earlier, on the tourists. Are you a Londoner?'

'I was,' said Victor Harker. 'I left London in the twenties. I've lived in Newcastle for fifty years.'

'I was never stationed in the north.'

'Where *did* you serve?'

'Serve?'

'In the army.'

'Ah, serve. "Serve" in the sense of "serving" King and country. And Queen. One mustn't forget the Queen, God bless her. I follow your meaning.' After a pause, he said abruptly : 'All over. I served all over. Except the north of England. You said you were in France?'

'Yes.'

'I was in Belgium. And Africa. All over Africa. Nigeria, mostly. I remember one time – I remember it vividly, vividly – when I and my platoon, plucky chaps, were outnumbered ten to one by the fuzzy-wuzzies. They were coming at us from every direction. Did we panic? No, sir. Co-ordination, you see. Discipline. I pride myself that we sent the wild-looking so-and-so's off without too much loss of life. They were screaming as they came at us, and they were screaming as they fled – it took a practised ear to tell the difference between the two noises the crazy buggers were making. Hal let his men have a night on the town after that little skirmish. Ah yes, Africa ! The heat !'

'Africa must be very hot.'

'It is. Worse than it is today. It's hot over there. Excessively so.'

'But beautiful, I imagine. I should like to visit a national park or a game reserve. I planned to go to Kenya this summer, but events decided otherwise.'

'Was I ever in Kenya? I suppose I must have been. A very colourful part of the continent, I seem to recall. Lots of flowers ; animals. Exotic.'

Victor Harker saw himself with Stella. They were in a car, which a smiling African was driving across a vast plain. Cheetahs flashed by.

'I shan't go now.'

'Duty calls.' The captain stood up. 'I must drag the ageing carcass back to work, I'm afraid. If there's a gullible foreigner waiting to hear what Saint Erconwald did in his spare time, then I'm his man, I'm his man.'

Victor Harker believed in first impressions. Shaking hands with Captain Standish in the cathedral, he had thought : I would never have allowed this man an overdraft ; he has the forced confidence of the untrustworthy ; his eyes are far too bright ; I shall try to avoid further conversation with him.

He had talked with him, though ; and he had listened. He had even accepted the captain's invitation to dine that evening at a restaurant 'for the discerning few'. Why had he been so glad, so eager to accept? A need for company, anyone's company — was that the reason?

A month ago he would have had no reason.

'None at all.'

Only a month ago Stella was alive.

The 'discerning few' were certainly a strange bunch
— they liked their meat stringy, their vegetables
dyed, their salads occupied by garden insects. The
wine that met with their approval made one's liver
flinch.

'That was delicious. Thank you.'

'I knew you would enjoy yourself here.' The
captain belched. 'I shan't say pardon. A release of
wind from the upper region is the finest compliment any diner can pay the chef. You weren't
embarrassed by my eupeptic outburst, I hope?'

'No,' Victor Harker lied. 'Not at all.'

'There are those present who feel differently. The
oddly dressed pair to our left are puce with disapproval.'

'So I see.'

The captain raised his voice : 'A man who has
fought for his country as bravely as I have can surely
be excused the occasional trifling breach of etiquette.'
He belched again. 'All clear now. I forced that one
up for their benefit, and a strain on the old pipe it
was, too, to tell the truth. A tot of Boney's brew will
repair the damage. You'll have one, of course?'

The captain ordered two brandies from a hovering
waiter.

Between sips of cognac — which came in a glass
that had not been warmed — Victor Harker heard
himself explain why he had returned to London. He
was a widower, he said ; he had locked up the house
he had shared with his beloved wife because

everything in it – chairs, cups and saucers, pictures, books ; everything in it – suggested some scene or other from their past. The happy memories were the hardest to bear.

And so here he was, at the end of his life, in the city of his birth. Mrs Harker – who had been with him to Venice and Rome, to Amsterdam and Prague – had never set foot in the capital. He was here – if it made sense to the captain, which it probably didn't – because he hated the place.

It made sense. 'Everything makes sense,' said the captain, 'and so does nothing. It depends on your point of view.'

Victor Harker, not understanding, stared at his companion. 'I think I know what you mean.' He was beginning to sound drunk. He had always been a moderate man : Stella, seeing and hearing him now, would not have recognized her dear, cagy husband. 'My Victor watches his words.' He hadn't watched them tonight. They'd poured from him, one after another. It was time to stop the flow : 'I wonder how long this drought will last.'

'Ask the A-rabs. They're used to them.'

'I don't understand you. Which Arabs ?'

'The ones who are besieging our capital city.'

'I haven't seen any.'

'How long have you been here, my friend ?'

'Only a day or so.'

'You'll see them. Before the week's over, you'll see them. You'll see the buggers everywhere. You'll begin to think you're in a suburb of Port Said. Suits,' he said menacingly, 'will soon be out-numbered by burnouses.'

Victor Harker, amazed, said nothing. His bewildered look prompted the captain to further explanation:

'They shit.'

'We all — er — defecate. It's common to everyone.' He added, to clinch the matter: 'Kings as well as chimney sweeps. The highest and the lowest.'

'True, true. But how do *they* shit — the A-rabs?'

'Is there a difference in the way they defecate?'

'A pronounced one. Not the actual function, obviously — the bowels must open, that they must — but the manner in which they do it, that's where the difference lies. They're what I call wayside shitters. They don't flush the stuff down holes, as we do. They leave their deposits anywhere and everywhere. Did you know that A-rabs hold the turd sacred?'

'No. No, I didn't.'

'Well, they do. That's why they leave it be. For them, it's a gift from above, not an inconvenience from below. I think they think it has a soul.'

Here I am, thought Victor Harker, listening to this man of winks and belches, this stranger whom I would never have trusted with an overdraft; here I am, in London of all places, listening to him as he tells me what I do not wish to know, and scarcely believe — that the Arabs worship the waste their bodies discard. Why, why am I listening?

'Even the confounded weather's turned A-rabian.'

'Yes.'

The captain called for the bill.

'Allow me to pay my share.'

'I'll allow no such thing. When I invite a pal out to dinner, I don't expect him to part with his money.'

'You must let me return the compliment one evening.'

'That I *will* allow.'

Outside the restaurant, the captain took Victor Harker's arm. 'I'll see you to your hotel.'

'It's only a few streets away. It's in Covent Garden.'

'The city's full of hooligans. You don't know London as I do. I insist.'

On the steps of the hotel they shook hands, and were about to part, when the captain said, 'May I ask you a personal question?'

'We're barely acquainted.'

'Can you still get it up?'

'It?'

'Your joystick. Your –'

'My – ?'

'Precisely.'

Victor Harker's laughter seemed to satisfy the captain.

'No need to answer. You're fighting fit. A credit to the regiment.'

Why had he laughed?

'Why did I laugh tonight at that question of his? Why didn't I take offence? Why didn't I tell him to take a running jump off the nearest bridge?'

Now he heard – in a pink-tiled, sweet-smelling bathroom – the echo of a laugh that had shaken his body on a field in France. It had sprung from his throat. It had leapt from him, wildly. It had had a will of its own.

He saw again, dimly, the cause of his cackle. The

smoke cleared, and George Popplewell emerged. George's whole face was gone – only blood, and bits of bone, and brains were left. George stood for a moment before his laughing friend, and a sound like water gurgling in a pipe escaped from him. George fell then – where others had fallen, and were to continue falling, all that long hot day.

Victor Harker pressed a bar of lavender soap to his nose. Soon George's stink was gone, and the echo too.

He would amuse himself tomorrow, looking for burnouses.

Two

The man who often called himself Captain Standish turned into Bow Street and strolled in the direction of the Strand. It was too late to claim a bed at the Mission : that fierce Sergeant Marybeth would have slammed the doors shut some hours ago. She admitted no one, not even her beloved Tommy, after ten o'clock.

He took off his blazer and loosened his tie. 'Shall I call a camel, or shall I walk?' The temperature was barmy, rather than balmy : he almost expected to see palms sprouting. 'It's worse than a Turkish bath.' Did Arabs, or A-rabs, take Turkish baths? Who knew? Who cared?

It was a long trot to Victoria, but his captain could rise to the challenge : he hadn't had a fainting fit in months. If he didn't rush, if he maintained a steady pace, his sprightly warrior would reach his destination – Mrs Hunter's lodgings. By the time he got there, the captain would be in need of a spot of shut-eye. 'I am not the man he was.'

He had lived with the captain nearly half his life. He had brought him into being – Harold, his first invention – out of boredom. The captain had been a major to begin with, then a colonel – until his creator had come to his senses, and decided not to be too ambitious : majors and colonels were relatively famous ; they could be traced. No one cared about a mere captain. A captain was neither high nor low in the officers' ranks – he was a man in the middle. A captain wasn't anybody ; he was a somebody, of sorts ; he was decidedly not a nobody. The bored inventor had settled for a captain.

'Bear up, Hal. Walking's good for the ticker. Keeps the carcass trim.'

He and the captain had had some larks over the years. Between them, they had kept the enemy at bay – that scourge of endless afternoons, overcast mornings, and lonely nights : Archbishop Tedium, Milady Languor, le Comte d'Ennui. Standish and he had woken up in all manner of bedrooms – functional (the sole necessity) ; rural (a cow dopily looking in) ; palatial (chandeliers ; Persian rugs ; a harpsichord) – in all manner of places. He had taken his soldier of fortune into houses where the rich and famous were regular visitors.

At Whitehall, he commanded the captain to pay his respects to Charles the First – the monarch who had had such rotten luck at the hands of that Bolshie brute, Cromwell. Standish stiffened before the statue and saluted. Some passing youths laughed at him and made whistling noises. 'You owe your lives to me,' he told them proudly.

'Thanks a lot' was the politest of their replies. Forming themselves into a straight line, they became privates on parade. Arms swinging in unison, they marched to Trafalgar Square, and then broke ranks. They laughed again ; they whistled.

'Disrespectful young bastards.'

He watched them, in his captain's ramrod stance, until they were out of sight.

In love? Victor Harker? It didn't make sense. The only passion dusty Mr Harker felt was for what he took home in his suitcase. It defied all reason, his clerk said — the idea of hard-faced Harker with his heart askew. Harker in love? Harker taking the plunge? Harker a husband? What a laugh!

'Congratulations, Mr Harker.'

'I don't understand you, Mason.'

'It was in the paper, sir. This morning, sir. About your engagement, sir. To Miss Palmer, sir.'

'Well, thank you, Mason.'

'Miss Palmer looks very pretty, Mr Harker.'

'She is, Mason. She is.'

She was. The beautiful Stella Palmer was a 'catch', and he — incredibly — had caught her. Meeting her had been his greatest good fortune. He had thanked the hare in his delight.

Mason's astonished features were before him as he lay, naked and sweating, on his hotel bed. He'd known what Mason had been thinking.

'I am a lucky man, Mason. I consider myself most fortunate. Where are those figures we discussed yesterday?'

'Here, sir. All in order, sir.'

'Have they startled you?'

'Sir?'

'The figures?'

'Oh no, sir. As I say, sir, they're all in order, sir.'

What had startled Mason, what had startled all his colleagues, was the fact that he, Victor Harker,

24

had fallen in love with a woman who was his junior by sixteen years. What was more startling to them, what had really sent their eyebrows into their forelocks, was the unlikely fact that she, Stella Palmer, apparently returned his feelings.

'My darling cagy one.'

How many times had he insisted, laughingly, that caginess wasn't in his nature?

'Hundreds of times.'

Nearing Victoria Station, where so many changes had taken place, the captain was assured by his inventor that Tommy's and Julian's clothes would stay in their respective lockers. He'd been promised a night at Mrs Hunter's, and that promise would be kept.

Mrs Hunter knew Captain Standish well. As Mrs Richards, she had known him in the biblical sense, but without the begetting. During their liaison, the late Mr Richards had never been mentioned, let alone mourned. These days, however, she took widowhood seriously – mementoes of Mr Hunter, including an urn containing his ashes, adorned the vestibule of her guest house. When the captain breakfasted with Mrs Hunter, it was not Mrs Richards who poured his tea. That lady was as good as buried.

'Which is fine by you – eh, Hal?'

Of course it was fine by Hal. Sleeping alongside Mrs Hunter, in the bed that had once bounced and creaked beneath the transported Mrs Richards and her skilled transporter, Hal was like a boy again. He felt Mrs Hunter's warmth, and she his, but as a

brother his sister's, a sister her brother's, in that
blessed state before the onset of puberty. She wore
her nightgown, he his pyjamas, and only their hands
met. They were as passionate as the figures on some
medieval tomb. This innocent union, all frenzy long
gone, suited Hal fine.

Occasionally, when the mood was on him, he
summoned up the strength to tackle a tart. Whores,
deceivers ever, had to be manoeuvred : you had to
keep a trick ahead of them. They knew how to
wriggle and whoop and get the performance over
almost before it had begun. Their customers — the
shy, the drunk, the strange — seldom questioned
them, seldom complained. They shot, and bolted.
Not Hal Standish, though ; no, not he. That still
impressively upright gentleman liked a run for his
money ; a good long ride on the swings and roundabouts. Hasty withdrawals were for the physically
bankrupt — the ones without reserves. He was, as
yet, not of their number.

'The girls used to pay *you*, didn't they, Hal ?'

'Not *girls* ; never *girls*. They were ladies. Most of
them had Honourable handles to their names. And
nothing as common as cash was pressed into my
discreetly withheld hand. I was rewarded for my
efforts in a manner befitting them. Ah, those handsome cheques, from such exclusive banks. And those
charming gifts !'

He cursed the discerning few as he made his fifth
trip to the bathroom. He cursed Captain Standish as
well. But mostly he cursed Victor Harker for be-
having out of character and making the acquaintance

26

of a man he would never, never, never have allowed to get in the red. In his retirement, it seemed, he was mixing with crooks. He was a world away from Stella now.

'Stella,' he said, to remind himself, in his humiliation, of the life they had shared. 'Forgive me.'

Sleep, when it came to him at last, led Victor Harker, dressed for business, into a church of sorts. It was a little like St Paul's and a little like a mosque. The service began. Great chords sounded on the organ, and the congregation rose. A thousand – at least a thousand – voices praised Him in the firmament, and in Newcastle, and in the Old Kent Road. 'Hosanna! Hosanna!' they sang. 'Hosanna in the highest!'

To his surprise, he was singing with them. Handel would have enjoyed the noise he was making – it was exultant, it was florid, and it seemed to be in tune. His heart was in the music: he felt it leaping, and dipping, and resting, and then leaping again – it did whatever the notes dictated. He looked about him to see if Stella was appreciative, but she wasn't there.

Captain Standish was. He was conducting. He was not pleased, he told him, that Victor Harker was working his way through the *Messiah* when everyone else was trying to come to grips with the *St John Passion*. 'It's rank insubordination – that's what it is, Harker. I have no alternative but to report you.'

He was still dodging sacred turds, dropping from a serenely blue sky, when he awoke.

'Marmalade, Hal?'

27

'Thank you, Joyce.'

'Your appetite's healthy, in spite of the heat.'

'I'm used to foreign climes, remember.'

'Forgetful me. I like to watch a man eat. That's the only thing you have in common with Mr H. – your way with a plate of food. He, too, left the china spotless.'

'He had a palate as discerning as my own, in that case, Joyce.'

It was a predictable response, but a welcome one: Mrs Hunter relished the captain's compliments. Then he surprised her by saying:

'In all the years I've known you, Joyce, you've never mentioned Mr Richards.'

'I had reason not to, Hal. If I can be said to have a motto in life, it is Look on the Bright Side. Mr Richards did not inspire me to bright thoughts, I'm afraid, and he doesn't do so now. I'm well aware which of the two places he's gone to, where I'm sure he's a welcome guest. I thank God that first you, and then Mr H. – though for so short a time – came along to cheer me up. Between you, you gave me a few hopes to cling on to. I had fun with you in my naughty days, and security from him. By and large, I would call myself a fortunate woman.'

'Is that all you have to say about him, Joyce?'

'You *are* curious this morning, Hal. Yes, I really do think that's all I have to say about him. He wasn't like you, Hal. He was a devious individual, not to be trusted.'

'And you trust me?'

'But of course. You're as open as a book to me, Hal Standish. I know where I am with you.'

The man who sometimes called himself Captain Standish expressed his old soldier's gratitude to Mrs Hunter for her faith in him. It gave Hal's maker enormous pleasure to reflect that this decent, amiable woman considered her former lover to be honest, to be — delicious idea — 'open'.

She cut his after-breakfast cigar for him, and told him, as she always did, to let his stomach have a proper rest before she ran his bath. While he read his *Times*, she would see to it that the lodgers were being attended to. The new Spanish maid was prone to unruliness. There had been the odd complaint.

'A sign of the pickle the country's in, if you ask me, Joyce.'

'Oh, you dear sweet silly. I've had temperamental staff in the past. Don't you recall that frightful girl who did a flit with my best cutlery? I haven't employed a Doris since.'

Hal had had a bit of sport with Doris, but he didn't say so. Her frightfulness had not been confined to the thieving of knives and forks.

An hour later — his first meal of the day safely digested — he thanked Mrs Hunter, as he usually did, for scrubbing his back.

'Your skill has not diminished, Joyce.'

'I must buy a fresh sponge before you come again, Hal. Four days, will it be?'

'Most probably, Joyce.'

'It worries me when you're not regular. Harm can come to a man your age — even to a healthy chap like Hal Standish. Which clothes shall I lay out for you?'

'The blue pin-stripe, if you'd be so kind.'

'In this weather, Hal? You'd be cooler in linen. Why don't you wear your what I call "tropical" suit?'

'Yes. Why don't I?'

Captain Standish, a vision from the time of the Raj, gave Mrs Hunter the customary chaste peck on the forehead, and promised to return unharmed. A man both rested and refreshed, he strode purposefully towards Victoria Station.

Once there, he soon vanished.

Victor Harker ate dry toast and drank China tea in the hotel restaurant. He saw no burnouses. What he did see saddened and horrified him — an elderly German wearing lederhosen. The man's legs were a mass of popping veins : trickles of purple and blue, of red and black, surrounded knotted cords. The man seemed unaware of the parasites feasting on his once handsome limbs — for him, they were handsome still. He stroked them whenever his hands were free. He looked at them with obvious pleasure. His wife eyed them with approval too.

Victor Harker turned in his chair. Odd, he thought, that I should be so near to the old enemy on this day of all days. It was the first of July. Sixty years before, he and hundreds of other soldiers had leapt into action after months of waiting. Victory had been assured ; the plan of campaign was foolproof. Nothing could possibly go wrong.

The laugh with the will of its own was evidence to the contrary.

Three

Tommy, jostled and pushed aside by hurrying travellers, took his time climbing the stairs. When he finally emerged from the lesser of the station's two lavatories, he stopped for a moment or so to catch his breath. Then he slouched across to the twenty-four-hour depository, where he left a linen suit, a white sea island cotton shirt, a silk tie, a pair of woollen socks, a pair of rayon underpants, and a pair of suede shoes — the lot to be collected at a later date. He also entrusted to a station locker a paper bag in which he'd placed an immaculate denture consisting of seven teeth — 'an upper set for one of the upper set', as its owner was fond of saying. The young man who checked these items in wondered how it was that such posh possessions could have come into the hands of the scruffy old sod who stood smiling at him.

'What's in the bag?'

'Teeth.'

'Teeth?'

'Not mine.'

'Not yours?'

'No. They belong to a real gentleman. I look after them for him when he goes away.'

The young man was surprised by the pleasantness

of the tramp's voice, by its refinement. There was only the faintest hint of Cockney in it.

'You'll treat them carefully, won't you?'

'That's what I'm paid to do. Here's your ticket.'

'Thank you kindly.'

Tommy shuffled off. Vast, sprawling, sweltering London awaited him : that city in which he had eked out an existence so different from Captain Standish's charmed life. Not for him the company of the manicured and the upholstered – Tommy's kind were the barely human ; the ones whom respectable people pretended did not exist. Tommy was out of the majority's sight, out of their minds.

Things were going well, were going (to coin a word) outstandishly, when Tommy came into being. His creator, anxious to be challenged, had begun to be just a trifle bored with his one impersonation. Constant bedroom manoeuvres were starting to take their toll : a change, he reasoned, would be as good as a rest. Walking briskly down Piccadilly one day – he was late for lunch at the Ritz – the captain was approached by a spectacularly filthy beggar to whom he tossed an appropriately stained sixpence. The captain's creator saw Tommy in an instant – a refined vagrant, quietly spoken, living on his un-demonstrative wits in the great metropolis.

Weeks later, Tommy made his first appearance. His air of faded respectability tore at many an anonymous heart. Here was a man who had definitely come down in the world : someone who had tried to make the climb, and failed. He wasn't a natural misfit, a born excrescence. His look had none of the manufactured humility that is more offensive to a sensitive person than open hatred. It was a dignified expression. It apologized to society from a respectful distance.

Over the years, Tommy had met some of the luminaries of his tribe. They had lightened, after their fashion, the London murk. It was sad to think of the ones who had been snuffed out : Lambeth Joe – who used to cavort through the borough with his pet rat, Alphonse, which he kept on a lead – was long under the ground, and Aggie the Bible-basher was dead, too. They had won his unreserved admiration. He would never have dared to have been as stylish.

A few genuine aristocrats lingered on. Stop Press Arnold still adorned West London. Chiswick was Arnold's pitch, though he sometimes went slumming in Shepherd's Bush. Eight bundles of yellowing newspapers accompanied him wherever he ate or slept. They were heavy, and could not all be carried at once. Arnold managed two at a time. He walked a dozen or so yards along the street, and then set down his treasures – with great care and concern – on the pavement. He would stare at them fondly for a moment before he walked back for a further pair. His progress each day was slow. This infinitely patient man, whose love for the printed word could not be described as orthodox, had an eye for dog poop that was second to no one's. His bundles had seldom been soiled.

Olive, a constant presence in and around Regent Street, was an aristocrat of a different kind, and – as far as Tommy was concerned – a noblewoman best avoided. That doll-like little lady – her cheeks so lightly touched with rouge – knew words that, in Tommy's opinion, ladies were not supposed to know, as he had once discovered. He had wandered accidentally on to her pitch one afternoon, where his sad eyes had elicited a five-pound note from a troubled Jap. Olive's fury had astonished him. She had called him, he blushed to remember, a scheming cunt. (Just to hear the word in one's head was unsettling.) She would have his guts for garters, she'd shrieked, if he ever set foot where he wasn't wanted again. Contrite Tommy had offered her the nip's fiver, but Olive had refused it : 'I don't accept no fucking charity from no fucking scum.' (Gracious !)

The young found Olive's sweetness appealing. She was the world's Ideal Granny. The long-hairs who sauntered in and out of the bookshop in front of which she dithered saw her and instantly reached into their bags and sacks for notes and coins. Olive swayed gently to the Indian music (he guessed it was Indian because of the photograph he'd seen in the window of a fat fakir looking pleased with himself) that occasionally pinged and plunked inside. If you stood within spitting distance of the dotty old charmer, you could hear her singing under her breath : 'Ping ! Plunk ! Plunk, plunk, ping, plunk !' Tommy had not heard Olive's lyrics for months now. Captain Standish had listened to them recently, though, and so had Julian.

Tommy passed Overton's, where the captain often treated himself to a plate of oysters, washed down with bubbly or a superior hock. Tommy's taste ran to jellied eels and strong tea, which he consumed at certain stalls in the East End, and at an always overcrowded café near Arnold's territory. Eels and mashed potatoes had been the regular Friday evening meal during his childhood.

He turned left, in order to avoid the new Victoria Street of concrete and glass. It was no place these days for an old Londoner. He had tried imploring there (the word 'begging' was as distasteful to Tommy as the filth Olive resorted to), but without success. The people who worked in those eye-sores of buildings weren't proper people at all – they, too, were made of glass and concrete.

My life's over, thought Victor Harker. It began in September 1922 and it ended in May 1976. It's over now. I'm a shadow of the man I was.

'It's two pounds to see the show, mister.'

He did not hear the man who spoke to him. Nor did he see what he appeared to be looking at: the blown-up photograph of a naked woman with pendulous breasts. He heard only his own thoughts; he saw only dust.

'I said it's two pounds to see the show, mister.'

'What show?'

'Beautiful girls. They do jig-jig. Very stimulating. Front row seat. Two pounds.'

The girl in the photograph was not beautiful. She smirked – and besides, her eyes were dead.

'No, thank you. I was thinking of something else.'

'Don't be shy, mister. It's natural to want to look at pussy.'

Victor Harker said 'No, thank you' again, and walked on. He was in Soho, he realized. When he was young, the girls hadn't danced, if that was what

doing jig-jig meant. They had done their bargaining
in the streets – under lamp-posts, in doorways. Their
brightly painted faces had frightened him. He had
felt no urge to kiss a mask.

He had stared at the women as if they were creatures in the zoo – tigers, flamingoes. Their jabber,
high and shrill, was as strange as the song of exotic
birds.

Billy Harker had availed himself of their services,
his son learned one night. Victor's mother had not
long been dead. Billy, drink in hand, had reached the
boastful stage in his evening monologue. He inten-
ded no disrespect to his dear Mary's memory, he
said, but a red-blooded man had more needs than a
wife could satisfy. A prostitute made it her business
to know what those needs were. No self-respecting
husband would expect his better half to throw
herself around like a common doxy.

Billy mentioned the names of the doxies who had
satisfied his needs. There was one called Fifi – she
was French, and had ooh-la-la. His Vic would
appreciate Fifi. The next time he visited her, he
would take his boy along.

After the boasting came the inevitable fit of
gloom – no one cared a damn what happened to
Billy Harker. He wished he'd had Mary's luck.

'You call that luck, Dad? You call pain luck?'

For answer, he received a snore. He poked out
the meagre fire and left his father asleep in the chair.

'I wish you *had* died,' he said as he went to the
room he shared with his sister, Lizzie. 'And I wish I
wasn't here.'

In Warwick Street, where he now found himself,

there was no sign of sleaziness. He walked into the Church of Our Lady of the Assumption. It was as cool a resting-place as he desired. He sat down. He did not think of God there, as he should have. He thought instead of those human beings whose belief in Him inspired the building of such retreats.

He left two pounds in the box for gifts and altar flowers.

Tommy was very partial to a cheese or ham roll, but since the departure of his front teeth, eating crusty bread was a difficult business. Mario, seeing him enter the café, asked his favourite *girovago* the usual question :

'You want the cheese or the ham today, *amico* ?'

To which Tommy, smiling, gave his customary 'Italian' reply, accompanied by 'Italian' gestures with the right hand :

'Today I want-a the-a cheese-a I think-a, Mario.'

Mario, whose own front teeth were filled with gold, laughed loudly. *'Tu parli bene Mediterraneo, Tommaso.'* 'Mediterraneo' was Mario's word for Tommy's 'Italian', a language the old man spoke best after drinking two or more bottles of beer. Because the café was not licensed to sell liquor, Mario served Tommy pale ale in a teacup.

'It's a day for *birra*, Tommaso.'

'I understandare,' said Tommy with a wink.

Mario placed the cup on Tommy's table and returned to the counter, where he gave Tommy's roll the special treatment of the house. He cut it in two, and dipped each half in milk. He shook the pieces and laid them on a plate. He buttered them.

He hacked a thin slice off a hunk of sweating Cheddar and stuck it between the bits of softened bread.

'*Al dente*,' he said to Tommy as he handed him the roll.

'No, Mario. *Alla gengiva*.'

The joke had been made more times than either man could remember. Mario had said '*alla gengiva*' first, after seeing Tommy, a new customer, take a lump of blood-soaked roll from his mouth: 'I make it soft for you. I make it *alla gengiva*.' The phrase was Tommy's now. It belonged to his other vocabulary.

'My *gengivas* are sore today.'

At noon, the café suddenly filled up. The place attracted a mixed clientèle: clerks, labourers, even ballet dancers in tights. One of these last – a plumpish girl with eyes as soulful as Tommy's – recognized a kindred spirit in the tramp and slipped him fifty pence.

'So kind,' he murmured. He picked up the plastic bag that contained his worldly goods, and with many an 'Excuse me' and 'I'd be obliged' he managed to negotiate a path to Mario, who was calling to his daughter for assistance.

'What-a is the-a damagiario?'

'How much you have, Tommaso?'

'Twenty.'

'Then you pay me ten pence.'

The meal was free more often than not. A ten-pence payment meant that Tommy was in the money.

'Take care, Tommaso. *Arrivederci*.'

'And Harry V. Dirtcheap to you, Mario.'

In a public garden that had once been a graveyard, Victor Harker saw a man drinking silver polish. The wretch sipped the mauve liquid fastidiously, savouring each drop. It gave his fascinated observer a strange feeling of comfort to reflect that Billy Harker, who had sunk so low, had somehow avoided the absolute bottom of the pit. If this man wasn't already there, he was as close to the brink as one could imagine : he was hardly more than a step away.

Perhaps Billy Harker had been lucky after all. Had he lived longer, who knows what depths he might have descended to? He had made his exit at the right moment.

Victor Harker remembered how his father had cried out to be taken from 'this vale of tears'. (Despite his lack of education, Billy knew a few fancy phrases.) In February 1922, his cries were heard. The 'flu epidemic that had raged through the poorer areas of London for most of the winter suddenly laid its claim on the life of William Ewart Harker. His removal a certainty, he screamed to be spared. In his delirium, he even promised to take the pledge.

No, Billy hadn't made an exit – nothing so positive. His manner of dying was entirely typical – a great deal of whining, followed by unconsciousness. The night of his death was much like any other in the Harker household. The only novelty was the fever that had caused Billy to sweat and gasp for breath.

What relief Billy's son had felt after the removal; what a sense of freedom. Fifty-four years later, on a hot, hot day, he saw his young self walking against the rain to the undertaker's. He'd had the fore-thought not to smile as he was ordering the coffin.

The barely human, not the aristocracy, were waiting outside the Mission. Tommy, exhausted by his long walk through the City, joined the line of down-and-outs in the late afternoon. Some stood; some swayed; some were sprawled across the pavement. They were bronzed to a man this summer: many a boozer's flush was already tanned mahogany. The dirtier ones, whose acquaintance with soap and water had never flowered into a lasting friendship, were nearly as black as the wall they leaned against. You'd have to aim for the whites of their eyes, thought Tommy's creator, forgetting for a moment that he wasn't Captain Standish.

Only a couple of the skulking forms were familiar to Tommy. One greeted him with an unsteady bow; the other wondered if he had anything in the kitty.

'Just the price of a night's sleep.'

There was no denying the honesty of Tommy's reply, which his questioner interpreted as 'If I had a penny more, I'd share it with you.' Tommy had been generous with his spare pennies on several occasions.

The trusted tramp inspected his companions in distress while he killed the hour or so before the Mission's doors opened. 'It's the dregs today,' he told himself. 'And they're young dregs, too.' The length of skin and bone standing beside him – in a

suit wide enough to contain another, more substantial, body as well — was nibbling at a nipple for
nourishment a week ago from yesterday.

There was, thanks be to God (Whose praises he'd
be singing tonight), no sign — or whiff — of Horace.
Tommy, who had eaten and slept alongside speci-
mens of humanity a fly would be choosy about
buzzing past, was averse to Horace's company. He
more than smelled — he stank. His breath stank ; his
feet stank ; his fingers and thumbs gave off vapours.
To be within a mile of him was to risk contamina-
tion. Thank the Lord he chose to rest his foul old
body in the London parks when the summer was
summery.

Horace had been forcibly washed in recent years.
In Middlesex Hospital, where he'd been taken after
collapsing in Charlotte Street, they'd had to cut him
out of his clothes. Six strong orderlies, the story
went, had had to hold him down. It was like trying
to land a whale, and a smelly one at that.

The doctor who examined the scrubbed Horace
discovered something that alarmed him. Horace had
syphilis. That in itself was no surprise — what was
amazing was that it was a new infection. He'd had
it no more than a week. When asked to name his
contact, Horace had replied with a snort.

Just to think of Horace and a woman doing the
act together made Tommy feel queasy. Was she
without a nose, this creature? Did she have eyes? If
she *could* see and smell, then what was the matter
with her brain? Why, and how, had she chosen
Horace for a partner? No one, except the 'lovers'
themselves, could answer these questions.

Tommy had never indulged in the act; had never wanted to. It sounded grubby to him – all that fiddling about down there. He thought it odd that men and women should enjoy themselves with parts of the body they used for other purposes. Unlike his fellow visitors to the Mission, he was a man untainted, untempted. Not for him a quick romp in the bushes, or up some alley, with a woman who gave herself for a cigarette or a swig at the bottle; not for his lips the filth he heard so often on the lips of his equals, spoken with such harsh relish. True, he said 'piddle' and 'poop', but the use of those two words from his boyhood was the nearest he came to swearing.

Skin-and-Bone appeared to be talking to him. He had to strain to listen, for only the faintest sounds were coming from the young wretch's mouth.

'Could you speak a little louder?' Tommy asked sweetly. 'My hearing's not what it was.'

'I feel cold.'

'It's very hot today. Are you ill?'

'I was warm a moment ago, but I'm cold now.'

Speaking seemed to exhaust the gangling youth: the last three words emerged in a whisper.

'Perhaps you have a slight chill. I'd ask Sergeant Marybeth for an aspirin, if I were you.'

Skin-and-Bone made no response to this suggestion. He smiled abruptly, but to himself. 'I'm warm again,' he said, and shivered. The arms of his ridiculous jacket flapped briefly.

Despite Tommy's determinedly easy-going efforts to engage him in conversation, Skin-and-Bone did nothing but nod and smile – always abruptly, always privately – until the Mission opened on the stroke of six.

Considering the food he'd eaten as a child – those scraps of meat that people today wouldn't throw to their dogs; those thin soups that got thinner as the week progressed – it was a miracle he was so fit. At the age of seventy-eight, he could still look at his body with something like pride. He had entered the world (his mother had fondly told him) a mere apology for a baby, weighing just under five pounds. She had feared that he wouldn't see the century out. She had even put money aside – where Billy couldn't find it – so that he might have a decent funeral, complete with mute.

What an unlikely survivor he was! He lifted his glass and drank a silent toast – the one he had said aloud in Stella's company every year of their marriage – to the memory of his friend George Popplewell.

That, too, was a miracle, a constant source of wonder: that Victor Harker had waited, and George Popplewell hadn't. He might have gurgled. George might have laughed.

Sergeant Marybeth, hands poised above the piano keys, watched as the last of her strays positioned himself at table. It was a Tommy night, which meant that the singing would be a bit livelier than usual. Her pet stray always put his heart and soul into the hymns. His voice was raw, but his feelings were genuine. He sang out with passion, his head high.

He sang out now. 'And Did Those Feet' was one

of his favourites. She could hear him, as she could not hear the others, calling for his Bow of Burning Gold and his Arrows of Desire :

> 'I will not cease from Mental Fight,
> Nor shall my Sword sleep in my hand,
> Till we have built Jerusalem
> In England's green and pleasant land.'

They couldn't build anything, her strays; they had stopped building themselves long since. Yet for Sergeant Marybeth, an old soldier in Christ, the idea of growth — of Jerusalem being built somewhere, somehow — was of paramount importance. Blake's words died in the men's throats, but they went on living. Her sword hadn't slept. While there was breath in her body, it never would.

Three Williams had enticed her to England: Shakespeare, Blake and Wordsworth. At school in Winnipeg, she had excelled in English literature. The forest of Arden, charter'd London, and Tintern Abbey were real to her in a way that the city of her birth wasn't — language, celebrating or denigrating their existence, had made them vivid. How often, during those endless Manitoban winters, had she longed to be with Rosalind and Orlando; beside the Thames; along the banks of the Wye. She had looked out at flatness, at snow, and summoned up greenness and grime.

In England at last, in 1936, she saw them both. It was not in the Lake District, but in Whitechapel, that she made the wisest, and most momentous, decision of her life. Other missionaries ventured into the jungle, into territory occupied by primitive

tribes, but she, Marybeth Myslawchuk, would fight
the good fight and spread the Word in the very
centre of Civilization. She could find enough darkness to combat in Leman Street, or in Cable Street,
where the harlots' curses rang out day and night : she
didn't need to wade through swampland, or to
endure malaria, to seek out the enemy. And anyway,
there was the weather to take into account. The
variable English climate suited her. In hygienic
Winnipeg it was either cold or hot, like the Ukraine
of her forefathers. She'd cabled her parents : HAVE
TO STAY IN LONDON. HAVE FOUND GOD AND JOINED
ARMY. DECISION IRREVERSIBLE. YOUR LOVING
DAUGHTER MARYBETH.

Yes, she had found God. She had believed in Him
before — but half-heartedly, and more from conven-
tion than conviction. She had found Him one damp
Saturday at Hyde Park Corner, in the voices of
some hungry men (unbelievers all, no doubt) who
had marched from the north of England to show the
politicians in the capital that if they weren't given
work, they would starve to death. The men's faces
were haggard and drawn, their mouths filled with
rotting teeth. They looked exhausted as they came
to the end of their long trek. Suddenly, a young man
with an old man's stooping shoulders called out :
'Let's sing 'em a song, lads !' Then the healthy
visitor from Canada heard, for the first time, Parry's
setting of Blake's poem on the tongues of a hundred
human scarecrows. She saw, through tears, the
healthy bodies they might have had ; that they would
surely have in the Jerusalem their singing invoked.

'Let us all say grace.'

Tommy and his companions mumbled, 'For what we are about to receive, may the Lord make us truly thankful' before sitting down to eat. Sergeant Marybeth — to her shame, she had to confess — was pleased that Horace and his cronies weren't of the party. They were probably carousing under a tree somewhere, ruining the remains of their livers with methanol.

Her thoughts were interrupted by a commotion at the table. One of her strays was shouting, 'Look at the way he's eating! Just look at the messy bastard!'

The speaker was a regular caller at the Mission, and one of its unworthier guests. He imagined himself a clown; he liked to mock, when he wasn't in a foul temper. It was his custom after a meal to bow his gratitude to Marybeth and the other soldiers, who had trained themselves to endure his waggery. He was screaming now: 'I tell you, it's an insult the way he's eating!'

'Oh, leave the boy be,' said Tommy. 'He means no harm.'

'I don't care what he means. He's putting me off my grub. It's criminal, the way he's eating!'

The object of the sarcastic man's abuse was a newcomer, a skinny youth in impossibly ill-fitting clothes, who was seated to the right of Tommy.

'Try chewing,' Sergeant Marybeth heard Tommy say to him. 'Try chewing and he'll shut up.'

'Sergeant, that funny-looking bastard's putting me off my food.'

'Our Father does not concern Himself with outward show. What looks funny to you is of serious concern to Him. If the young man is illegitimate – which I doubt, which I doubt very much – then that is God's plan. You may be illegitimate yourself, for all I know. You are still welcome here, in spite of your bad behaviour.'

'But look at the way he's eating, Sergeant,' the man whined.

The sergeant looked. She had seen better table manners. Shovel, shovel – the food was disappearing like so much rubbish. 'Why don't you take your time? No one's going to steal your dinner.'

The youth made no reply, no acknowledgment that she had spoken even. He continued shovelling.

'Pigs wouldn't let him near their trough.'

He picked up his empty plate and licked it clean. Then he drank a cup of tea in one gulp. Then he belched.

'You going to ask for more, Oliver Twist?'

Sergeant Marybeth was beginning to wonder if the gaunt young man were deaf and dumb. His large grey eyes, she noticed, had no sparkle in them ; they were focused, dully, elsewhere.

The Mission's jester – a Yorick to be forgotten, the sergeant thought – returned to his meal. 'Look, Oliver,' he said, 'this is the way a gentleman eats.'

On his way to the factory that cool August morning, Victor Harker stopped to read a poster. There were a good many words on it, but four alone brought him to a halt : 'A Call To Arms'. Above them was the message 'Your King & Country Need You'. Below them, in much smaller print, was the explanation. The sixteen-year-old Victor, a working man

47

already, studied it with care: 'An addition of 100,000 men to His Majesty's Regular Army', he learned, was 'immediately necessary in the present grave National Emergency'. Was it possible that he would be the first to enlist, or the hundredth, or even the hundred-thousandth? He read on, hopefully, until he came to the sentence that turned his hope into an idle dream – a dream as unlikely of becoming a reality as one of his father's promises: 'Age on Enlistment, between 19 and 30'.

In spite of his disappointment, he read the rest of the appeal. He was several inches taller than the minimum required height for a volunteer; his chest was broad enough, too: everything except age was in his favour. His seventeenth birthday was a week away; his means of escape was two whole years.

For that's what Lord Kitchener's plea meant to him: escape from London; escape from poverty; escape from Billy Harker and his widower's black tie. His Lordship, in his anxiety to protect the Empire, would send Private Harker to Fifiland, where women knew a thing or two, and frogs were eaten; where people spoke down their noses, and men wore berets and played accordions. In France, he could be someone different, someone new.

There was no way he could become Private Harker – none whatsobloodyever. He set off for the factory, disconsolate. At the gates he said to himself, 'I'm going to try, though. I'm going to try' and, turning, walked with a purpose away from the hellhole where he made candles for nothing-half-penny a week. The foreman shouted 'It's over here, Harker!' but the soldier-to-be ignored him.

He left Mile End, where everyone knew how old he was, and headed for Blackfriars. Once there, he went into a post office and asked a clerk for the information he needed. The clerk gave him a list of addresses and wished him luck in his fight against the Kaiser. Hours later – his throat parched; his feet aching – he arrived at White City, on the other side of London. The recruiting office was filled with men, some of whom were obviously toffs, for they wore overcoats with velvet collars and had hair that glistened. He had an old, torn cotton scarf around his neck, but they sported silk ties kept in place by pins. They stood together in a corner, at some distance from the group he joined. He knew where he belonged – among the heads that didn't shine; among the coats in tatters; among the shirtless.

'Come to the desk, young 'un,' said a recruiting officer. Billy's bold son did as he was ordered.

'How old are you?'

'Me?'

'Yes, you. I'm not looking at the cat's mother.'

The officer's remark caused the men to laugh. In his nervousness, his stupidity, the boy who wanted to go to war answered, 'Seventeen, sir.'

The officer was silent for a moment or two. Then he said, 'I didn't hear you correctly. I'm deaf in one ear, and that must have been the one that caught "seventeen". Let me give you a word of advice. Go outside, walk round the block, take a deep breath and come in again and tell me, and tell me loudly, seeing as how I have this problem with my hearing, that your age isn't what my bad ear thought it heard.

I want your proper age, young man, and make sure you give it to me.' The officer winked. 'Understood?'

'Yes, sir.'

On his return, the now calm recruit told the smiling man in uniform that he, Victor Joseph Harker, was nineteen years old.

'Of course you are. I never doubted you for a minute.'

He took the oath of allegiance to King and country; he promised to take up the word of Justice; he shook hands with the man whose bad ear had brought him good fortune, and went out into the street.

He would not tell his father, he decided; he'd keep his news a secret from Lizzie too. He would do his training and go.

Victor Harker, drinking brandy from a glass that had been properly warmed, remembered the meal he'd eaten on that momentous day. It was tripe and cowheel, and Lizzie had had to heat it up because he was late getting home.

Tommy fell asleep to the usual chorus of coughs, snores, belches and farts. It was past twelve before he lost consciousness. Skin-and-Bone, in the next bed, had been in the Land of Nod since the lights went out. He was having a good time there, to judge by his smile, which Tommy could make out in the half-light. He was still wearing his suit, even though Major Geraldine had entreated him to take it off. 'I'll see that no one steals it,' she'd assured him. All that he had removed, however, were his shoes and socks – the only items in his wardrobe that seemed to fit him.

Tommy's dreams were rarely Tommy's. They belonged to Captain Standish and Julian as well. The three personalities occasionally merged, to their creator's bewilderment. The three shared a nightmare. A man who had their face and their body was in a field. Vague figures – shapes of men, nothing more – were ahead of him. There were trees in the distance. He was unable to move towards them, although he wanted to. The sky turned red. His hands, his arms, his legs were incapable of movement. He was paralysed. When he tried to scream, his mouth wouldn't open.

He was gulping for air when he awoke. As soon as he realized that the dream was over, he asked himself who he was. The smells, the coarse sheets, the men – he was Tommy, and he was in the Mission.

In the half-light, he could see Skin-and-Bone's lips moving. He propped himself up, to catch what the boy was saying.

'...Oh yes, he was definite about it. The touch. He'd never known a touch as good as mine. Oh yes. He'd seen and heard them all and he knew. Practice, practice, practice – that's what he said. Eight hours at a stretch, and that's the minimum. Oh yes. One day I should be able to play concertos as well as I played that rondo. I had the right touch for Mozart – light, strong, firm, quick, oh yes. Oh yes, oh yes. England's answer to Schnabel, he said I'd be. Have you heard Clara Haskil? I sound like her at the keyboard. No effort, no effort at all, not a trace. You'd think the piano was playing itself. You'd think Mozart was inside me – his ghost at least. You'd think you were in paradise. Oh yes. And not just Mozart – Brahms, Schumann. I love Schumann, I love his moods. He suffered. He felt pain. Oh yes. It's in his music; I feel it too, when I play. Look at my hands – how fine they are! Aren't they fine? Wouldn't you say so? You can see them at the piano, can't you? Oh yes. *Maestoso, adagio, allegro non troppo*. The fingers, the thumbs. Oh yes. I come out to the podium; I shake hands with the conductor. No, I don't. That's afterwards – at the end, after the last note has died away. Applause, applause. I can't hear it, because the music, the beauty, is still in my head. The conductor takes *my* hand and shakes it. He pats me on the back. "*Bravo, bravissimo*!" The violins, violas, cellos are saluting me: I see their bows tapping the stands. They know an artist when they hear one. Oh yes. I go; I come back; I go again; I come back again; I go yet again; I come back yet again, with the conductor, without him, on my own, solo, oh yes. A lady throws flowers. I pick them up. I sniff them. I am touched. I want to cry – from joy, joy. This is happiness. I am happy. I go, finally. He knew, even then, that I would play Mozart, Schumann, Brahms. I was six when he heard me. Six! A prodigy. A genius. Pianists are born, not made. Discipline yourself, he said. Practice makes perfect. Scales, arpeggios. Look to the future. Work, work. Treat your hands carefully, he said; they are your passport to a better life. Oh yes. He was right. I know he was right. I know he was right. I know. Oh yes. I know he was right...'

Skin-and-Bone's voice trailed away. There was

silence in the dormitory. Then Tommy's creator heard a sound that frightened him – a croak, a rattle. Was it, in heaven's name, the death rattle?

It was. Tommy, waking for the second time, saw Sergeant Marybeth and two male soldiers trying unsuccessfully to stir Skin-and-Bone into life. Sergeant Marybeth was wearing her fiercest look – one that indicated that the boy had offended her by dying.

'No luck, Sergeant. He's gone.'

'It's pitiful, pitiful,' she said. 'We'd best get him out of here before they all wake up.'

The Mission's jester had heard the rattle too, and had gone back to sleep. At dawn he'd got up to empty his bladder and on his way to the toilet he had passed the boy he called Oliver. The fixed smile, the hands clawing at the blanket – the mucky eater had the look of a stiff. He forgot his need to piss and went to the soldier on dormitory duty and told him that he thought the youth who'd made a pig of himself at dinner was dead.

Sergeant Marybeth said, 'He's so young, Tommy. He can't be more than twenty.'

'No, Sergeant.'

'These things happen.'

'Yes, Sergeant.'

'Don't let it upset you.'

'I'll try not to.'

Tommy's creator watched the men carry the boy in the ridiculous-looking suit out of the room in which no flowers had been thrown. Skin-and-Bone, he thought, is now with Mozart, Schumann and Brahms, among others. He found himself crying.

They lay – the man of forty and his bride of twenty-four – in that state of sweet exhaustion he had long imagined would be the aftermath of lovemaking. This is a tiredness, he said to himself, I shall always welcome.

His drowsy girl stirred in his arms.

'Stella.'

She stirred again.

'Stella, angel, pinch me.'

'Pinch you? Why?'

'To see.'

'To see what, silly?'

'If I'm really alive. If what's happening's happening.'

Four

Tommy evaporated at St Pancras and Julian emerged
from the station's lavatory. Julian Borrow, a poet
still unrecognized, lolloped along Euston Road, his
white hair hidden beneath a purple fedora. He had
as many teeth as Captain Standish, though Julian's
were crooked (a triumph of the dental technician's
art) and tobacco-stained. He looked grubbier than
Tommy, but classier : Julian's shirts, as threadbare
as those worn by the clean-faced tramp, were
interestingly, even artistically, splotched. Those
dabs of dried egg and ink, those red dots caused by a
hand that had an unsteady hold on a beaker full of
the warm South, suggested a man whose mind was
preoccupied with other than earthly things.

Julian had been born, so to speak, in the reading-
room of one of London's many libraries. Tommy had
gone there to read a bit and snooze a bit one rainy
afternoon. The place was crowded with shipwrecked
tramps, a rum assortment of castaways. Steam rose
from their ragged coats and trousers as they looked
through the *Tatler* or *Country Life*, keeping themselves *au fait* with the latest goings-on in Society.
Tommy, seated opposite a hairy Scot in a clinging
kilt who was reading a newspaper that bore the
headline RING OF BESTIAL SHEPHERDS EXPOSED,

turned his attention away from rustic wonkiness and concentrated on the more palatable stories that filled the pages of an already dampened *Daily Telegraph*. The suicide of a middle-aged man was reported in it. Alongside his body, Tommy learned, were the manuscripts of some thirty-five books he had written. Not one had been published.

'He's my next one,' thought Tommy's creator. 'He'll be a poet. He'll tax my powers, Julian will.'

The name had come to him instantly; the clothes had followed soon after — corduroy, of course, and sandals; in all weathers, those sandals. The Borrow wardrobe had been purchased by Captain Standish.

Julian's ivory tower was at the top of an early-Victorian house in Islington. Its walls were decorated with publishers' rejection slips — a positive No-play, Julian thought, of print and colour. The principal motif, constantly repeated from a variety of angles, expressed regret under the heading Faber and Faber. The room, to which the smallest kitchen imaginable was attached, contained a divan bed, a table, and a chair. It was warmed in winter by a gas fire that hissed, spat, and — at its hottest — yelped like an anguished puppy.

Unlike the other buildings in the street, Number Seventy had not been renovated or painted. Its occupants, of whom Julian was the longest-lasting, would have looked out of place in a spick-and-span residence. Seediness suited them. They belonged to crumbling Number Seventy as monks belong to a monastery. Their new, energetic neighbours resented the presence of this established order of mild eccentrics, who lowered the tone of a now fashionable area. They particularly disliked the old misfit in corduroy. They had warned their attractive children not to speak to him.

Julian had known many women. There are girls who specialize in poets, and some of them had sought him out. Julian's had names like Myfanwy, Hermione, Augusta, Chloe. They were none of them pretty, yet they weren't plain either. The word to describe their looks was 'striking'. They'd all doted on him for a time, especially the green-eyed Hermione, who had set several of his poems to music. Julian's lady-loves were expected to admire his art with unqualified enthusiasm. In return for the honour of being allowed to take part in the creative process ('Just seeing you sitting there, Deirdre, fills me with inspiration'), Julian agreed to their washing his clothes, cooking his meals, and entering his bed. They lacked expertise in all three activities, though they didn't know it. Sex with Augusta or Myfanwy was always a robust business; with Chloe it had gone beyond the merely lively into a state that verged on the gladiatorial. Where Captain Standish was master, totally in command, Julian was victim, the object of a desire almost too fierce to be assuaged. Hal brought his ship safely to berth, but Julian was lucky if his didn't capsize.

Victor Harker walked beside the stagnant Thames. He had no fixed destination. He would follow his feet for a while.

They led him across Tower Bridge and into Rotherhithe, where he stopped to look at Tower Bridge Buildings. Those dozens of poky flats, built during Victoria's reign, were considered fit dwellings for the poor once. He heard a voice from that time, no one's in particular; a common voice, sharp as scissors, saying to a woman who might have been his grandmother: 'The height of luxury it is, Lil; you should see it. Like a bleeding palace it is after what me and Bert's been used to. You'll have to put on your finery when you pay us a visit.'

The poor occupied the Buildings still. They were out on the balconies enjoying the sun, reading the papers, drinking and lounging. A child waved to him. Embarrassed, feeling like a snooper, he moved on: he was an intruder now where once he would have been at home. In one dingy street after another he sensed that eyes were following him. Curtains twitched as he went by: behind them were Lils and Berts, Sids and Flos, and a Billy Harker or two perhaps.

He passed a housing estate, a modern counterpart to the Buildings – characterless concrete instead of oppressive brick – which some wit of a town planner had honoured with the name Charles Dickens. A grim joke, he thought, that the writer who had informed the English of the existence of Jo the crossing-sweeper should be celebrated in this way. He wondered how many of its residents, their heads stuck in tabloids this Sunday morning, had read those books that Stella and Victor Harker had loved so much.

He was thinking about retracing his steps when he saw a church. A few elderly worshippers were shaking hands with the clergyman in the portal. He would wait for everyone to leave before going in.

He enjoyed churches when they were empty, and empty for him meant free from vicars and curates and wardens. He had never cared for men of the cloth – their breeziness gave him the shivers. He loathed their clockwork optimism. He hated that pitying look they assumed, that instant recognition of one's supposed fallen state. In his years of darkness he had needed the places they strutted in, not them.

Soon after entering St Mary's, Victor Harker fancied that he was in the presence of simple goodness. Wives had prayed here for the safe return of their sailor husbands, not heeding the carvings by Grinling Gibbons and the splendour of the organ. They were mere decorations : the progress of those ships across the Atlantic or the Pacific was what mattered. 'You *are* being fanciful,' he told himself, and yet he couldn't shake off the conviction that the atmosphere in this dockland church was suggestive of centuries of quiet, undemonstrative devotion. What grandeur St Mary's contained lay in its unoccupied pews, where ghosts now sang for him :

> O hear us when we cry to Thee
> For those in peril on the sea.

Hesitant voices were still singing faintly as he read the plaques on the walls. His notion seemed less fanciful with every dedication he looked at : a woman called Everilda Bracken had come from Sutton Coldfield to the shipbuilding village of Rotherhithe 'to relieve the sufferers from the cholera' ; a certain Roger Tweedy, who died in 1655, decreed in his will that the sum of two shillings be distributed 'every Lords Day forever among twelve poor seamen or their widdows in bread', while other widows, of good character only, were remembered in the bequest of a Mr John Sprunt. He learned that Prince Lee Boo, the son of the ruler of the Pelau Islands, had died in Captain Wilson's house in Paradise Row in a smallpox epidemic. The captain had been shown great kindness by the prince's family when his ship, the *Antelope*, was wrecked on the shores of the Pelau in 1783...Once again he saw hands clawing the air, and gold and brass wedding-rings glinting on the water.

'On Tuesday, yes.'

The face of the man he would never have granted an overdraft had suddenly appeared above the wreck of the *Antelope*, or was it the H.M.S. *Captain*? It must have been the latter he was thinking of. Captain, Captain – he and that Standish individual had arranged to meet for dinner the day after tomorrow. Victor Harker would take his guest to a restaurant which the discerning few neglected to patronize.

Wandering back along the wharves, he tried to picture the prince, who had left somewhere like paradise only to die in a street on London's out-skirts that bore its name. Had he worn grass, or feathers, or both? Victor Harker thought of the captain's wife, who had not been widowed young, substituting sensible wool and cotton for the prince's showy clothing.

'He died of a fever, and no one could save him, and that was the end of poor Prince Lee Boo,' he sang under his breath.

The man who sometimes donned the poet's mantle
nibbled at a late Sunday breakfast of kippers and
Dundee marmalade. He had been upset since
Friday morning, when he had heard a sound in the
stuffy Mission that had frozen his old body — no
part of him had escaped that swift, icy clutch. He
wondered, as he manoeuvred a fish bone out of
Julian's denture with a newly sharpened pencil, who
would hear that sound when the time came for him
to make it.

He removed Julian's teeth and dipped them in a
glass of warm Spanish Chablis. Before returning
them to his mouth, he freshened his palate with the
wine : gargle, rinse, swallow. When Julian was
complete once more, and could speak as Julian, the
poet reminded himself that he had better be wending
his way or he would be late for his lecture.

The scourge of all things modern picked up his
orange box in the hallway and checked the angle of
his fedora in the hallstand mirror.

'On with the show, Julian. There's life in you
yet. Make them listen.'

It was no easy task, making 'them' listen. Few of
'them' were interested in poetry — they were there
for a laugh ; they were there to idle away a summer
afternoon. They would be there in a swarm today,
as they had been since April, like so many insects
buzzing happily in the heat. He, Julian, would
silence their noise.

Mopping sweat from his face with a handkerchief that wasn't spotless, the aesthete entered a pub
near Marble Arch. He liked to imbibe before

standing up for his beliefs : a drop of the nectarous beverage always added a glow to his performance. He ordered a carafe of white wine from a barman dressed in Tudor costume, who responded to Julian's 'What Elysium have ye known?' with a baffled 'Bloody tropical and that's a truth, mate.' Sensing that an explanation of his question would only elicit another comment on the strangeness of the weather, Julian lit his pipe and waited while a barmaid dressed as Nell Gwynn cleared a table for him. He resisted the temptation to inquire after His Majesty's health and simply said 'Thank you' to the comely wench when she removed the last of the debris. 'She'd do for Standish,' thought Julian's maker.

Julian drank, and puffed, and puffed, and drank, and nothing like a glow took hold of him. His thoughts were all of death : death in the Mission, death in the street, death right here in the here and now in the Mermaid Tavern – he might die any-where. Mrs Hunter and Sergeant Marybeth and Julian's ageing girls would all shed a tear for him. A sudden stab at the heart, a sudden explosion in the head – let it be quick when it comes ; let it please be quick, said the voice inside.

The men's lavatory, he noticed, was Ye Knightes, the women's Ye Damsels. He was joined in Ye Knightes by Sir Francis Drake, who said, 'Bloody tropical and that's a truth, mate,' as he unzipped his unTudor fly. 'Yes, it is strange weather we're enduring,' said Julian. 'It's bloody tropical, that's what it is,' continued the Armada's scatterer. 'If you want my opinion, I'd say it was bloody tropical.'

Julian said good day to the swashbuckler and returned to the saloon bar. He lifted his fedora to Mistress Gwynn, who honoured him with a brief smile. He picked up his box and went out into the street. The sunlight dazzled him. Minutes passed before his eyes became accustomed to the glare.

Standing on his box at Speakers' Corner, he surveyed the crowd: the usual oafs were milling about; the usual predatory pederasts were waiting to pounce on some spotty Ganymede. He cleared his throat and began. Poets, he told a man with a tic, are a special breed; they are above humdrum humanity; they inhale a finer air. Parnassus is their common country, whatever their place of birth.

The man with the quivering nostril was now joined by two elderly women and a fat American with a camera perched on his belly. Soon Julian had a substantial audience.

The poet, Julian asserted, is a privileged creature. He is a connoisseur of language – his every word is as a note in music. Today's poets, if one could call them such, had forsaken the Parnassian slopes – where sweet rivulets sparkle yet midst verdant pastures – for the coarse clay of the mundane modern world. The Grecian urn had been replaced by the teapot and the beer bottle, neither of which vessels had the fearful symmetry to inspire a true disciple of Apollo to thoughts of immortality. Muck, filth, slime: these were the properties of contemporary verse. Today's poetry, if that's what it was, contained no Light, no Beauty, no Music, no Wonder. Yes, yes – Wonder, the sense of Wonder, of the

63

wide world being Wondrous and Wonderful, that sense was missing.

'What do you think of T. S. Eliot?' asked the man with the restless nose.

'Not for nothing, my friend,' Julian replied, 'is his name an anagram of "toilets". Need I say more?'

'I'm afraid so, yes. If you claim to be an expert and a poet, then you do need to say more. And I am not your friend.'

'A manner of speaking. One says "my friend" as a manner of speaking.'

'That seems to be all you're doing – speaking in a rather mannered way.'

'Aha, a critic! I know the breed. Too well do I know the breed. You have a critic's air about you, my friend who prefers to be my enemy. You scorn, you mock, you sneer. You stand outside Parnassus – indeed, you are forbidden entry, since critical trespassers will be forever prosecuted – and you envy those who have passed beyond the gates and drunk at the divine springs.'

'As a plumber I know all about springs, divine or otherwise. I'll give you my card – just in case you ever have trouble with your celestial waterworks.'

The crowd laughed. Julian glowered.

The American photographed the angry old kook for his collection of English eccentrics.

Leaves were already falling from the trees, and the grass that should have been green was already turning brown. If I see a burnous here, thought Victor Harker, I won't find it out of place. The park was as parched as any desert.

A year ago he and Stella had taken what was to be their last walk together. It had rained that morning. The earth was still wet as they made their way, hand in hand, towards Howick. Larks, in abundance, had risen before them — each brief song making a sweet contrast to the perpetual squall of the gulls swirling above the calm North Sea. They'd rested on the beach, among the ochre rocks and grey buckthorn, where they'd had their last picnic.

He saw his dear girl, her eyes on the ocean; he heard her say, 'It was a lovely idea, this little trip. You've always been thoughtful, as well as cagy.'

In the hospital, three days after their little trip, he'd promised to take her to Africa. 'We'll go on safari, angel. But only on one condition.'

'What's that?'

'That you get better.' She'd managed a smile. 'Soon.'

She was nowhere now, and he was in the park, in London, alone with hundreds of sprawling bodies.

Leaving the densely occupied desert at Marble Arch, he decided to stop and hear what the speakers had to say. A sober Billy had brought him to this poor man's parliament on a rare excursion from Mile End. Two outings to Margate and a day with his father seeing London's sights — such were his childhood holidays.

A man was prophesying the end of the world; another, to all appearances tattooed from bald head to foot, was showing a delighted audience how he had escaped from Sing Sing, Dartmoor, the Santé, Devil's Island, Wormwood Scrubs — and every prison ever built, it seemed; a Methodist minister was explaining why socialism was the only political doctrine that squared with the teachings of Christ; an immense Negro was calling for revolution in Rhodesia – and someone who looked like Captain Standish was pretending to be indifferent to the abuse with which his speech was being received.

Victor Harker listened. The captain's double was talking in riddles – a whole lot of guff about eternity, and the soul, and the wonderful, wondrous universe. His voice, so unlike the captain's, was constantly on the verge of song; his words, and there were many of them, were being tra-la-la'd, not spoken normally. The man laughed at one point, and Victor Harker saw teeth that bore no resemblance to the disconcertingly white snappers the captain sported.

Julian waited until Captain Standish's dull new acquaintance was out of sight before he brought his lecture to a flamboyant close. 'Let the welkin ring and the fancy roam,' he advised his listeners, who broke into mocking applause when he stepped down. 'More, more,' said the plumber, his nose in a frenzy. Julian looked at him with distaste and replied, 'I have given you quite enough to think about.'

He slept fitfully that night. Each time he awoke he drank from the wine bottle at his bedside. He was no longer Julian, although he was in Julian's room, surrounded by Julian's junk. He was himself, whoever that was; he was the man in the field, the man in the common nightmare. He was the paralysed man for whom the distant trees were rattling, rattling.

Five

The house was gone. In its place, fittingly, was a shop selling wines and spirits. It was licensed to a Mr S. Patel. Victor Harker wondered if his father's ghost hovered over Mr Patel's bottles, unhappy that it couldn't drink.

J. Patel owned the obligatory supermarket, F. Patel the dry cleaner's. I. Patel had a bakery; N. Patel sold papers, tobacco, and sweets. A large tabby cat slept in the window of a run-down establishment where somebody did little or no business in trimmings. Behind the dirty glass were six dusty balls of wool, a packet of needles, and something pink that looked vaguely surgical. There was an air of defiant decay about the place, as if it were a last bastion against the invasion from the tropics: its inadequate ammunition would not keep the enemy at bay for long. The lone, anonymous haberdasher who lurked in its shadows, refusing to concede defeat, was surely possessed of an insane courage.

'Senile dementia, Victor Harker. You're letting your mind wander.'

He remembered the shopkeepers of his childhood: surly Harry Long, the butcher; Mrs Atkins, in the corner grocery, who allowed her friend, the long-suffering wife of Billy Harker, to put a quarter-pound of tea or a piece of cheese on the slate when money was scarce; 'Whiskers' Edmunds, the only bearded man in the street, who stuffed animals – your dear old dog; your budgie or canary – for what he called a 'reasonable remuneration' – there was no trace of them now. Now the wheel of Empire had been spun arsy-versy: the turban seemed to be as common a sight here as the cloth cap he himself had worn as a youth.

Whose smile was he returning? S. Patel's? J.'s? N.'s? He was tempted to ask. He walked on. Not many years ago, he thought, that Indian might have salaamed before me. To him I'd have been – what was the word? – a sahib. He would have shown me – if only for the colour of my skin – a respect as unwelcome as it was undeserved. All that pandering palaver belonged to history now.

Victor Harker reminded himself that he was in the East End for a purpose – if purpose it could be called. He had respects to pay – if staring at a lump stuck in the earth meant paying respects. He saw a flower shop and went in. 'I should like some roses,' he said to a plump woman in a sari.

'I fear only hot house, sir. They are expensive. The drought is the reason for the expense.'

'I should like them, all the same. Six will be enough.'

'They are for a lady?'

'Yes.'

'How very charming. How very gracious. The lady will appreciate them, I am certain. I choose you the best I have. The cost is more high than usual because of the behaviour of the weather and that they are grown in hot house and not in open air.'

'They look beautiful.'

He was about to do what he could not, and would not, do for Stella. Stella had no grave. Stella had forbidden him even to think about putting up any such monstrous thing. Stella had said: 'You'll scatter whatever bits of me come out of the furnace, won't you, my cagy darling?' He'd scattered those bits. The wind had taken them where guillemots and seagulls dived.

Armed with roses, he entered the cemetery. People could see that he hadn't come to snoop.

'Senile dementia. Who cares why you're here?'

The place was not as he remembered it. It had been ordered once – now it was wild. Gravestones were chipped, or covered with moss, or broken in pieces. Some lay flat on the grass. A blackberry bush sprawled across several plots: its withering claws had an entire tomb in their possession. No one, clearly, could be bothered to free that once impressive monument – in black marble, wasn't it? – from their clutch. Who, in this of all parts of London, could have afforded something so large, and in marble too? The man must have owned a brewery, or a pub that did a roaring trade.

'All the pubs around here did that.'

Some children were playing football. Yes, it wasn't an illusion: some boys, white and brown, were playing football – or rather a version of the game, since there was only one goal, and its posts were graves. The young Smiths and the young Patels ran and leapt and kicked and scrapped, as unaware as animals that they were on consecrated ground. He stopped to watch them. They looked no older than ten.

One of the boys called to him: 'You got a daughter, mister?' Before he could reply, another boy said: 'He's old. He's a grandad.' 'You got a grand-daughter then?' asked the first boy.

'No.'

All but two of the players came over to him. 'You're lucky, mate, you don't have no daughters,' said a young Indian, in the sharpest Cockney accent.

'Why's that?'

The boys laughed. Some spluttered.

'You a stranger?' asked a second brown child, with eyes and teeth that shone.

'I was born near here, but I left a long time ago.'

'Well, mate, I'd say you was lucky because girls get done in Spooky Park at night.'

'Spooky Park?'

'This dopy dump. We call it Spooky Park, seeing it's like a park only it's got spooks. Girls get done in here of a night.'

More laughs. More splutters.

'Dirty sods hide in them bushes and wait for girls going home and then they grab the girls – ' The speaker, a white boy, demonstrated how a dirty sod made a grab – 'and then they – ' The speaker hesitated – 'sort of shoves it in.'

'Really?'

'Really and truly, honest. Girls get done and blokes get done for. One bloke had his guts cut clean out of him, my mum said. She see it in the paper so you have to believe her.'

'Yes, of course. Don't let me interrupt your game. I must be on my way.'

Victor Harker waved the boys goodbye. Where, in all this mess, this clutter, were his parents buried? He left the footballers' grove and entered a wilderness. He saw, in the distance, an abandoned chapel. He made towards it. A short service had been held there for the mortal remains of Mary, the beloved wife of William. From there, perhaps, he could find his bearings.

He wasn't looking for the grave when he found it. The chapel was still some distance away. The words 'virtues blend' — faintly visible on a blackened slab — made him stop. He asked himself why they should be familiar. They were part of the poem, that was why. 'Put a poem on it,' Billy had said to the undertaker. 'I want her sent off with some nice words.' Mr Groom had been only too pleased to put a poem on it.

Victor Harker bent down and peered at the stone. 'Virtues blend, virtues blend,' he mumbled. 'What was the rest of the damned thing?' Slowly, with the aid of his reading glasses, he deciphered Billy's heartfelt message, written by an unknown hand. 'Suitable. Very suitable,' Mr Groom had said.

As wife and mother, neighbour and as friend
She set example where all virtues blend
For her the husband, the children drop the tear
While all that earth could claim lies mould'ring
here.

Billy had dropped the tear; his children hadn't. Lizzie and Vic had stood on either side of their weeping father, embarrassed. They'd stared glumly as the earth thumped on the coffin. Lizzie had pointed at a fat worm wriggling from a spade: 'Do you see him, Vic?'

'Yes, Lizzie.'

(The worms he was to see in France. The rats he was to see there.)

He whispered now: 'Have these roses, Mother.'

He had to shake his right leg into life when he stood up. The roses were startlingly red – they blazed against the blackness. 'They'll last the day out, dear,' he said.

He hobbled across to Billy's plot. There'd been no poem for him: poems were pricey in '22, as pricey as angels, and besides there wasn't time that February, with so many sinking, said Mr Groom, to chip them out. And then there was the shortage of stone. The war had played havoc with the funeral business, Mr Groom had gone on to say, begging an old soldier's pardon. Makeshift memorials were what he had to settle for these days – makeshift memorials.

So Billy, like a thousand others, had been buried beneath a simple headstone with a wood surround. 'I could get you a poem knocked out in six months or so,' Mr Groom had offered. Billy's son had not been hesitant declining: 'No, thanks, Mr Groom,' he'd said. 'Just his name and dates will do.'

Victor Harker stared down at the makeshift memorial with its faded letters and numbers. He heard himself say: 'You made me what I am. You brought me Stella.' Billy had been the swamp across which he had built his fortress over the years.

Billy's hated whine had been a clarion call to him, waking him out of lethargy and defeat, spurring him into action. He had wanted to be anyone but Billy. Had he been like Billy, he would not have known love.

He returned to his mother's grave and took a rose – the largest – from the bunch. He placed it in front of the makeshift memorial. As a token of his reluctant gratitude? Perhaps.

'Senile dementia.'

His stomach growled and instantly he thought of Stella. He'd met her shortly before his fortieth birthday. He was at that time of life when a man becomes aware of his plumbing, when he wakes in the night to sounds of protest from within – joints creaking, intestines in a riot. Noises apart, he'd been healthier than most: others of his age had had to pant their way over the hill, whereas he'd made the climb without any trouble. His hair had begun to turn grey, that was all. He'd been a decent physical specimen, in spite of the food he'd eaten as a lad (those scraps, those soups) and in spite of the trenches. On the surface, at least, he was as well as a forty-year-old could be expected to be.

And his heart? His ticker, he'd learned from his doctor, was in regular order – no sign of strain; not a hint of pressure. What a shrivelled thing it was, even so. No wonder his clerk, young Mason, had called him dusty. No wonder he was considered cold. The seat of his affections had been heavily cushioned: the idea of tenderness – of arms linked, joys shared – had hardly occurred to him. When he had thought of marriage it had only been in terms of domesticity. He'd pictured a mate who would sew and cook and clean and be happy with a mere husband. He'd wanted, he supposed, a mere wife.

The 'catch' had liked to boast that she'd caught him. 'I saw you in your cage,' she said, 'and I knew I had to let you out.' He'd marvelled at his girl's percipience : she'd seen, immediately, the cause of his dustiness. He recalled the tears he'd shed on the day of their engagement – tears of delight ; tears of acknowledgment that the bars around him had collapsed.

'I've never seen a man weep. Father says that men should only cry in private. Don't stop, Victor. I know you're crying because you think you're lucky. It's me who's that.'

He was dry-eyed now. He had been dry-eyed since May. He quickened his step and, as he did so, tripped over a cherub that had toppled from a nearby monument – a far from makeshift memorial. He cursed mildly and then laughed. 'You've broken your wings, my little fellow,' he said.

He was senile and he was demented. He was also ravenous. He could eat a substantial meal for once. Tonight he would have something more than his usual frugal portion of meat or fish – he would order extra vegetables, some cheese, a dessert. He would gorge himself – within limits, of course.

'I'm so hungry, Victor, I could swallow a horse between two mattresses' – that was George Popplewell's expression. How George had complained about those helpings of stew or bully beef ! There was rarely enough of the swill to satisfy him. George had told his friend, Victor, how he longed to be

74

home with Violet, far away from the bloody worms and the bloody rats and the bloody bully beef. Violet was George's girl. George had a snap of her, a cheap card he kept in his wallet. 'Right next to my heart,' he'd said, with an apologetic laugh. Violet had watched the birdie, all right – she'd glared at Dicky and challenged him to fly away and not leave her likeness behind.

She hadn't glared when Victor Harker, back from the war to end all wars, had called on her to let her know that George had died bravely. He had meant to tell her that her fiancé had behaved like a hero, but found that his respect for the truth prevented him. There'd been no opportunity for heroism. He'd talked instead, with a lump in his throat that hindered speech, of what he owed to George. George had introduced him to poetry – he'd never read it before, not even at school. In those long months before the battle, George had often opened his tattered old anthology and read to him. George had been partial to poems about nature – did Miss Kemp remember?

'No,' she had answered, surprising him. He had waited for an explanation, but none was given. He'd said, to end the awkward silence: 'Well, it must have been because of France. The poems reminded him of England. Cuckoos, the greenness of the grass and the hedges – those things. Particularly the hedges. There were no hedges where we were. George used to say: "I miss those blankety-blank hedges, Victor." It was chalk soil, you see. There were trees, of course, but they were a long way in the distance.'

'He mentioned the trees in a letter. Do have some walnut cake.'

'Thank you.'

She hadn't glared and she hadn't smiled. When she said, 'I had to laugh at George's attempts at piano-playing. He hit one note in five,' there was no suggestion of pleasure in her voice or on her face. He'd felt embarrassed. His eyes had avoided hers – they'd settled on the brass-topped table between them, on the delicate teapot that was so unlike the dark brown monster on the Harkers' stove, on the transparent teacups patterned with pagodas; they'd settled anywhere and everywhere in that neat and tidy parlour. He'd been frightened of drinking his tea – his hands were all fingers and thumbs whenever he put the cup to his lips. The mine, the blood, the gurgle – how could he mention such horrors when he was scared of dropping a piece of china and shattering it in two?

After several more awkward silences, he'd stumbled to his feet. 'I must be going' – the cliché that signalled rescue had come easily to him. As he left the room, he noticed with relief that the tea set was intact.

'It's two years since his death,' Violet had said with sudden earnestness as they lingered on the step. 'I don't want to forget him, Mr Harker. I never shall. Please understand. I'm grateful that you came to see me. I don't want to forget him, but I have to forget what we might have had. I wish to live in the present.'

'Yes. One must.'

'I can't be Mrs Popplewell now, can I?'

76

'No.'

'Miss Kemp thinks you're a gentleman. Miss Kemp was touched by the way you substituted "blankety-blank" for George's favourite word.'

She'd dashed back into the tidy house, closing the door with its stained-glass panels behind her.

He was on a train bound for the City.

'Senile dementia.'

He had been with Violet on the down escalator and on the platform. He had been with her, he realized, for most of his journey.

He hoped, as he had hoped before, that she had changed her name.

The man who often called himself Captain Standish wore Standish's best silk pyjamas as he lay awake in Mrs Hunter's bed. 'It's good to have you here a whole day earlier than usual,' she'd remarked after giving him his goodnight peck. 'It's an unexpected pleasure.'

Mrs Hunter was warm, but he was not. Her hand in his was clammy. He thought of the figures on a medieval tomb and shuddered. He didn't want to think of tombs, medieval or otherwise. He didn't want to think of tombs at all.

What an absent-minded oaf he'd been that afternoon! He was a mere matter of yards away from Mrs Hunter's when it occurred to him that something was wrong with his appearance. What was it? Not his clothes, certainly: from crown to sole he was Hal to the life. A convenient coughing fit provided him with the answer, as Julian's teeth joined a dollop of phlegm in the captain's handkerchief.

He'd had to hurry back to the station to effect the changeover.

Tomorrow evening the Standish pearlies would get to grips with a juicy fillet; a quiche; a runny, smelly Brie. That old fogy from Newcastle, as he'd expected, was going to take him to a decent restaurant. Hal's ruse had worked: Banker Harker's voice on the telephone was proof of that. The man was out to impress him. Tomorrow evening Captain Standish would be eating the best Frog food in London.

In the meantime, he was cold.

Six

Victor Harker sipped dry sherry while he waited for his guest. He was tired after a day of church-going – the red plush around him was restful to his eyes. Dense darkness within, fierce light outside : that afternoon he'd strained what Stella had called his gorgeous blue orbs to their uttermost.

He looked at his watch. The captain was fifteen minutes late. I shouldn't mind if he didn't turn up, thought Victor Harker. I'd be perfectly happy if I never saw the untrustworthy old so-and-so again.

'Apologies for the tardiness. I hailed taxi after taxi, but every one was occupied by swarthy persons in robes. As a result I was reduced to travelling on the underground with the odds and sods and assorted riff-raff. I'm most frightfully sorry.'

'That's all right. It's good to see you. You'll have a drink ?'

'A Scotch and soda would be agreeable.'

The whisky was brought, and the captain raised his glass. 'A toast to the patient host,' he said. Victor Harker, embarrassed, responded quickly : 'Yes, yes. Thank you. I do hope you approve of my choice of restaurant. I have to say that I like the look of it. It's a long while since I was served by waiters dressed as penguins. Their black tails and starched shirtfronts inspire confidence.'

'Ah, yes. A breath of the past.'

'I don't sigh for the dear dead days very often – only occasionally, and only for certain things. I didn't eat in a good restaurant until I was in my thirties. My stomach resisted at first – it wasn't accustomed to anything richer than stew. It still resists food that's too heavily garnished.'

'It couldn't be more different from Captain Harold's tum-tum, then. He's pleased to inform you that his reticulum, so to speak, is a mechanical marvel. He has taken it to the best tables, where it has acquitted itself proudly. I don't suppose you remember Romano's?'

'No.'

'Hal does. He remembers Romano's well. It was in the Strand. There were four floors. Hal was a regular patron – when he was on leave, of course.'

'Places like that were beyond my pocket. I used to stop outside them and stare in. Then I'd go home to scraps.'

'You poor fellow.'

'That's exactly what I was – a poor fellow.'

'Hal's had to rough it at times, too. Were you ever in India?'

'Never.'

'Hal was. He really roughed it in Calcutta. Terrible hell-hole. You wouldn't have enjoyed being in his shoes. Not in Calcutta you wouldn't have.'

'Probably not. By the way, I haven't seen any burnouses.'

'Burnouses?'

'You said I would see them everywhere in London.'

'Oh yes. So I did. I saw several this evening, all in taxis.'

'I haven't seen any. I saw plenty of turbans, though.'

'You did?'

'Yes. Sikhs, I assume.'

'Most likely. Keep on the alert for burnouses, Harker — that's my advice. Be ever watchful.' The captain winked. 'Report to H.Q. with your findings, like a trusty soldier. Reconnoitring is of the essence.'

'I think we might order.'

'An excellent suggestion.'

This man is insane, thought Victor Harker. I am merely demented, but he is well and truly round the bend. Why am I entertaining him?

He heard the captain tell the waiter: 'What I'd really welcome is some *lièvre. Lièvre rôti.*'

'We have no frozen food here, *monsieur*. It is our custom. If you wish to eat our *lièvre*, you must return in October when it is in season.'

The captain muttered 'Alas and alack' and said that he'd begin with *quiche lorraine* and follow that inimitable custard with *filet en croûte.*

'And *monsieur?*'

'*Monsieur*', who had not been called *monsieur* in sixty years, replied that he would like the *pâté de la maison* and, for his main course, something very simple but succulent — what would the waiter recommend?

'The *épaule d'agneau, monsieur*. A shoulder of lamb, delicately flavoured with marjoram and thyme, roasted with potatoes. *Monsieur* will find it very much to his taste, I guarantee.'

The wine waiter, whose black coat had a green sheen, appeared from nowhere and advised the gentlemen to try a Fleurie that had just arrived. His voice had a sepulchral authority — it was not to be argued with.

'London has changed a great deal,' said Victor Harker when the waiters were gone.

'And for the worse. Definitely for the worse.'

'I hardly recognize it any more. You leave a place and expect it to remain the same. It stays fixed in your mind's eye : nothing and no one can alter it. Then you return, and the alterations shock you.'

'They do. I well remember how they shocked me when I came home from India. It took me weeks to make out the lie of the land.'

'Yesterday I went back to the East End. That's where I grew up. I'd forgotten about the last war, about the Blitz, about those streets reduced to rubble. I remembered only the poky little house I was born in and the poky little houses around it. They've gone. And the candle factory I once worked in — that's gone, too.'

'It must have been an upsetting experience.'

'It wasn't. Not at all. It wasn't at all upsetting. The part of London I knew best as a boy was nothing to marvel at. They say as you get older that the past becomes more attractive, that you see it in a rosy glow. Not in my case. It's never looked rosy to me, my young life. It wasn't warm at the time, and I can't think warmly of it now. Except for my mother, that is.'

'Ah, yes. There is no woman in this world quite like one's mother,' said Captain Standish with what struck Victor Harker as a curious lack of conviction.

'Exactly. I was barely grown when she died. Afterwards, after she'd been put in the earth — You're not ill, are you?'

'Fit as a fiddle.'

'Your hands are shaking.'

'Regular occurrence. They'll stop in a jiffy. Go on with what you were saying.'

'After my mother's death, I took to visiting churches. All kinds, all denominations. I'm not a religious man — although my wife used to say you would have thought I was if you'd seen me listening to Handel's *Messiah*. No, I've no patience with God or gods, or what's above and what's below. I've always believed that it's here — *terra firma* — that matters. I must have been a strange lad. I had no real friend until I went to France. He was blown to pieces on the Somme.'

'Poor blighter.'

'Yes. Yes, indeed. As I say, I must have been strange. I would spend whole days in churches. It was their coldness and their darkness — those were the things that gave me comfort. St Paul's was a second home to me.'

'Hal has a soft spot for the stately pile, too,' said the captain before toasting Sir Christopher Wren with the dregs of his whisky.

'I went into some of his others today.'

'Whose others?'

'Wren's. Four of them. I started with St Benet, where I hit my shins when I tried to sit down in one of the pews. Talk about narrow! The congregation must be hardened – at least, I hope they are. They're Welsh, so they should be. Then I visited St James on Garlick Hill, which looks as if it's been restored. I was bewildered by it as a boy. Churches were made of stone and wood, outside and in – not iron. I found all that iron frightening – iron columns, iron sword rests, iron hat-stands, the whole caboodle. There was no reassurance in iron. Years later, in France, I learned to think differently. I was polishing my bayonet in anticipation of the great day – the day on which the score would be settled, and the Boche would be taught their lesson – when it suddenly occurred to me that the metal would be clean before it stuck in a man's guts.' He paused. 'Am I talking nonsense?'

'My goodness, no. Not in the least. Why do you ask?'

'I wondered. I've always been sparing with words, you see. I've always been wary of talking too much. I distrust talkers. I distrust myself when my tongue's loose. That's why I asked.'

'You were on the subject, if I recall correctly, of iron.'

'Yes, I'm afraid I was. I was saying that I was in France. Oh, it sounds absurd now. I was cleaning a bayonet, nothing more. The damned thing was gleaming by the time I'd finished with it. Why was it gleaming? Why had I made it shine? Because I was obeying an order to keep my equipment in working condition – '

'Protocol. Very important. Has to be maintained, protocol.'

'Yes, yes. You're right. Even so – '

'Come, come, Harker. No insubordination in the ranks,' said the captain, winking.

'Even so, Captain Standish.'

'Hal to you.'

'Even so, Hal.' He hesitated slightly before saying the name. 'Even so, I remember thinking : what difference would it make to my victim if there were rust on the blade? This afternoon, in St James's, that memory came back to me : how, as I was polishing, I'd pictured the inside of that same church, and said to myself, "That's the way metal should be used. It should be used as stone or paint is used – to create something beautiful." As I say, it sounds absurd.'

'Here's our starters. In the nick of time.'

'Yes. I'm peckish, too.'

They began to eat.

'Scrumptious,' said the captain.

'I'm so glad. I wonder if the wine has breathed sufficiently. You'd like some, wouldn't you? I know I would.'

'Capital idea.'

Again it was from nowhere that the wine waiter appeared, and at the very moment that his services were needed – his voice emerging from what Victor Harker fancied was a blackened, mossy tombstone.

'Senile dementia.'

'I beg your pardon, sir?'

'Oh, nothing. I was muttering to myself.'

'That way – it is said, sir – madness lies,' said the

waiter, with the approximation of a grin. 'Would you care to taste the wine?'

'I think my guest here should do that. I'm no expert.'

'I'll be happy to test the nectarous fluid – to borrow a phrase from an old chum.'

The waiter poured a small measure in the captain's glass.

The captain sniffed the wine, tasted it, smacked his lips and said, 'My compliments to your shippers.'

The waiter filled their glasses and vanished.

'To your lasting health, my new-found friend,' said the captain.

'And to yours.'

They returned to their meal.

'I don't know if it's the weather that's affecting me,' Victor Harker said, 'but I saw your double on Sunday.'

'Impossible. There's only one Hal Standish. The world isn't large enough to accommodate two of him. Where did this illusion happen?'

'In Hyde Park, at Speakers' Corner. You – I mean the man who bears a resemblance to you. *He* was standing on an orange-box talking a load of guff about eternity and the universe. His voice was not a bit like yours; he might have been singing. He wasn't well-dressed, and his teeth were filthy.'

'I expect they still are.'

'Of course.'

'In what way, precisely, did he resemble Captain Standish?'

'You?'

'Eh? Why, yes. Me.'

'His face.'

'He has my eyes, does he? And my nose?'

'From where I was standing, that's how it seemed.'

'Amazing. Truly amazing.'

They watched in silence as the plates were cleared.

'I had such an appetite yesterday,' Victor Harker announced. 'I could have eaten a horse between two mattresses.' He waited for a response, but none came – not even the inevitable wink. He wanted to talk about George Popplewell. He continued: 'I don't eat much, as a rule. I don't need to. But yesterday, in the cemetery – '

'Cemetery?'

'Cemetery, yes.'

'I don't see a connection.'

'Forgive me. I'm confusing you. What I'm trying to tell you is that it was in a graveyard, of all unlikely places, that I felt hungrier than I have in years – positively ravenous. The odd thing was, though, that when I returned to my hotel I could eat no more than my usual small portion – what my wife always called my sparrow's share. And eating that required an effort.'

'Amazing,' said Captain Standish as the man inside him caught a glimpse of distant trees and shuddered.

'Are you sure you're well?'

'Me?'

'Who else? There's no one else sitting opposite.'

'Why, yes. Yes, I'm perfectly well.'

'You looked for a second as if you were shivering.'

'Regular occurrence. They're fairly regular, I

regret to say, those sudden spasms. Age, I fear. I try not to let them bother me.'

'Have you sought medical advice?'

'The day has yet to dawn when you'll find Hal Standish consulting a quack. Why should he worry about the occasional spasm?'

'You said they were regular.'

'Regular, yes, but not frequent – that's why I said occasional. The captain is hunky-dory in every department, right down to his prostate. Is yours functioning, Victor?'

'I assume so.'

'Good man, good man. Long may it thrive!' The captain drained his glass. The wine waiter manifested himself and refilled it.

'I think, perhaps, we may need another bottle,' Victor Harker suggested.

'I had anticipated that contingency, sir.'

'Thank you.'

The wine waiter gave a half-bow and vanished. He was replaced by two younger waiters wearing, Victor Harker noticed, younger coats. They set the main course on the table with elegant efficiency before they, too, disappeared into the recesses of the restaurant.

'To our respective prostates,' exclaimed the captain. Victor Harker was both amused and embarrassed. They clinked glasses. 'And now let battle commence. Let us wage war on the enemy – food. Eradicate him, Private Harker, eradicate him.'

'This lamb smells delicious.'

'See how juicy my steak is. And how light the pastry.'

'I seem to be all memories tonight. Sitting here, I'm reminded – believe it or not – of the trenches. Can you guess why?'

'Haven't a clue.'

'I'm reminded because we privates often talked about our generals wining and dining in their *châteaux*. No rats came out for a peep while *they* were gorging themselves. They weren't stuck in the earth. We'd picture them in their armchairs, nursing their after-dinner drinks and puffing on their Havanas, and we'd hope they'd choke. Does what I say offend you?'

'I'm offended that you ask. A captain, my friend, is a man in the middle. He's neither high nor low. He isn't a major, and he isn't a corporal, and he most certainly is not a general. There were no *châteaux* for me.'

'I do apologize. I should have realized – '

'I'm not saying that Hal never saw the inside of a palatial residence, mind you. He did. He sat on the Sheraton in his heyday, and drank out of the Waterford. But not when he was on active duty – not then. Ask any of the old soldiers who served under him. They'll tell you that Hal was always there, in the thick of things. Hal the man of leisure and Hal the man of action were two very different creatures.'

'I'm sure they were.'

'Don't be *too* sure.'

'I'm sorry, I – '

'My joke – or, should I say, a joke at the captain's expense.'

'I don't understand.'

'Naturally you don't. You could hardly be expected to. You cannot lay claim to being an expert on the rare life of Captain Standish.'

'I only met him — you, that is — last week.'

The captain's empty glass was refilled, and a little wine added to Victor Harker's.

'A fortunate encounter, eh?'

Victor Harker hoped that his 'Yes' sounded enthusiastic.

'If our paths hadn't crossed, we wouldn't be sitting here. A man must have company.'

'Were you ever married, Captain?'

'Hal.'

'Hal. It always takes me time to get on friendly terms with people. Were you ever married, Hal?'

'No. Had the opportunity to marry, obviously. Had several opportunities to. Didn't think it practicable, though — marriage. Couldn't expect a woman to follow me to — ' He stopped. 'To follow me to — ' He seemed unable to speak. He stared glassily at his host. Then he winked.

'To follow you to?'

'You haven't been to Africa, have you?'

'No.'

'To follow me to Africa.'

'What about India?'

'You're quite right. India, yes. Couldn't expect her to follow me there either.'

'Many women did. Follow their husbands.'

'I know, I know. Officers' wives. Met some of them. Had a bit of sport with a general's lady once. On the whole, however, it has to be said that they're an ugly lot. Plain Janes all. Faces like Derby winners.

Voices that put icicles on your joystick. The captain didn't wish to be lumbered with one of those. He valued his freedom too much.'

'I had a fine marriage.'

'Lucky man.'

'I am. I was. We were the best of friends.'

'The two of you heard, I presume, the patter of tiny feet?'

'No, we didn't. We wanted to, but we didn't. All our attempts to start a family failed. A boy was born to us prematurely during the last war. He lived for three days.'

The captain said nothing.

'Ours was a quiet life. In the evenings, when I'd done with my office work, we'd listen to music on the gramophone — the Busch Quartet playing Schubert and Beethoven ; Horowitz's Chopin — '

'And Schumann? Did you listen to Schumann?'

'His songs.'

'And Brahms?'

'The symphonies.'

'Not the concertos?'

'Oh, yes. We played them frequently.'

'And Mozart?'

'How can one love music and not love Mozart?' He looked intently at his guest. 'You're shaking again.'

'Regular occurrence. Take no notice. It'll pass.'

'They're your favourites, are they?'

'Favourites?'

'The composers you mentioned.'

'No. Not at all. I like a band myself. Like to dance. Like to whoop it up. Lively tunes. Kind that set the feet tapping. I cut quite a figure on the floor, I can tell you. I can still trip the light fantastic. Oh, yes. Oh, yes.'

'I don't doubt you.'

The captain, reaching for the bottle of Fleurie, was intercepted by the wine waiter.

'Allow me, sir.'

'Happily.'

'I'll remove this old soldier if I may, gentlemen. The new recruit is breathing nicely.'

'A remarkable man,' observed Victor Harker when the wine waiter had once again disappeared.

'Quick on the draw. Quick on the draw.'

'Yes, he is.'

'Shakes have stopped – do you see? They just come and go – there's no telling when.'

'Let's hope they've gone for the evening.'

'I'll drink to that.'

'We read books together, too.'

'What?'

'My wife and I. Aloud. Dickens mostly.'

'I've been too busy for books. Somebody ought to write my life story. What a tale and a half that would be.'

'Why don't you write it yourself?'

'Haven't the patience. Or the skill.'

A salad was brought to the table and fresh plates set before them.

'Unlike my chum, Julian Borrow,' the captain continued. 'He and his pen are seldom apart.'

'I don't believe I've seen his work.'

'It hasn't been published, that's why. Obviously you haven't seen it. Myself and a few other privileged persons, all of them female, are the only ones who have. It would have been nothing less than a bloody miracle if you had seen it, that's what it would have been.'

'Why don't you persuade him to write your life?' asked Victor Harker with studied politeness.

'Impossible.'

'Impossible?'

'Impossible. I saw him yesterday for the last time. I left him at Victoria Station in a condition that I am tempted to describe as disintegrated. He's probably still there.' The captain laughed. 'In fact, there's no "probably" about it – he *is* still there.'

'I'm confused.'

'He is powerless without me. He will linger at the railway terminal until he is thrown away.'

The second bottle of Fleurie appeared before the captain, who said, 'This is better stuff than *he* ever drank,' as his glass was filled.

I shan't see this lunatic again, Victor Harker assured himself. I shall tell him I'm returning to Newcastle. I shall change hotels. I shall do my best to shake him off, as soon as dinner's over.

He saw that the captain was staring at him and smiling.

'You look pleased about something.'

'Do I? I was just thinking of another old chum, name of Tommy. I was just debating whether or not I'd have him meet his Waterloo at Waterloo. Stations are good places for farewells.'

'You have to say goodbye to him?'

'Oh, yes. You won't catch me seeing him off at the Mission. I've had enough of those wrecks. I'll meet him where I last left him, which was either Euston or St Pancras, and then I'll go with him to Waterloo. That, I predict, will be my plan of campaign.' The captain winked. 'Everything clear?'

'As mud. As mist.'

'Knew it would be.' The captain rose. 'I must go and use the telephone. Have some business to do — necessary business. I must also visit the room that's lined with porcelain. Shouldn't be any need to send out a search party. Order some Brie for me, there's a kind fellow. Hal likes it runny and smelly.'

The captain swayed into the darkness.

Victor Harker thought of Stella. Often, waking from dreams of the trenches, of George's mangled face or of Billy's hated whining, he would see her looking down at him, gently mopping his brow, murmuring, 'There, my darling. It's all over. I'm here.' He would love his angel girl then, with a tenderness that combated the horrors in his head and soon had them trounced.

'Stella,' he whispered. 'Why am I here without you?'

'You desire some cheese, *monsieur*?'

'My guest would like some Brie and I would appreciate a small sliver of Stilton. Blue, not white.'

What, indeed, was he doing here, parting with a small fortune for the pleasure of a maniac's company?

'Business settled. Bladder emptied.'

'I've ordered cheese. Would you care for a dessert as well?'

'I'll take anything you're offering.'

'I shall finish with Stilton. I don't have a sweet tooth.'

'There you're different from Hal.'

'We don't seem to have much in common.' Victor Harker heard the sharpness in his tone and did not regret it. 'I find it odd that we've struck up an acquaintance.'

'A man must have company.'

'Not necessarily. It's possible to live alone, with memories.'

'Is it? Is that what you're doing in London?'

Victor Harker had come to London because their house in Newcastle, his and Stella's, with its view over the moor, contained chairs, cups and saucers, tables, curtains, knives, forks, spoons — ordinary things; shared things; things that tore at his heart. Each of those ordinary things was an emblem of her absence.

'I came to London,' he said eventually, 'for a short while, for a change of scenery. I shall return to Newcastle in a day or so.'

'That's a pity. That's a terrible pity.'

'Are you serious?'

'Yes, Victor, I am.'

Victor Harker, rendered speechless, hoped that his companion would oblige with the dreadful wink or the hollow laugh. Nothing had ever seemed so false to him as the captain's praise. He wanted some confirmation of his feelings. The wink, now, would be most welcome.

The waiters arrived and provided distraction — they cleared the cheese plates, brought the dessert trolley for the captain to drool over, and poured coffee. The last of the wine went into the glass that had held most of it.

Fresh figs were the captain's choice.

'You'll drink some cognac with me?'

'With positively no persuasion, Victor.'

The waiters vanished. The captain referred to the healthy state of his bowels and began to eat. Victor Harker, watching him, wondered how he could steer the conversation in a sensible direction.

'What was it that you asked for earlier in the evening?'

'Eh?'

'When we were ordering dinner. There was a dish you asked for. You were advised to return in October.'

'Now I'm on your wavelength. It was *lièvre*.'

'Could you translate?'

'*Avec plaisir. Lièvre* is Frog for hare.'

'The animal?'

'What else?'

'A stupid question.'

The creature leapt, and stopped, and leapt again, and then it turned and ran back the way it had come. Victor Harker watched its mad dance. He glimpsed its distracted eyes and saw its suspicious ears shoot up. 'My future is going to be bright,' he told himself when he was left with only ragwort to look at.

Hours later, the train wound round the bridge into Newcastle. His first impression was of soot – even the river Tyne seemed stained with it. Every building was black. The setting sun was coated with a dust that had turned it purple.

'I've never eaten hare.'

'Hal adores anything gamey.'

96

The cognac was served in glasses that had been properly warmed.

'I have another toast to make,' said the captain. 'It is my sincere wish that we will meet again.'

'It won't be soon, I'm afraid.'

'Perhaps not. Let us greet the occasion anyway. To our next jolly get-together!'

'Yes. Yes.'

'Whenever, and wherever, it will be.'

'Walk a straight line, Hal, or you'll be spending the night in the copshop.'

The man inside Captain Standish halted beneath a lamp and consulted his old soldier's watch. There was nearly an hour to kill before his assignation. He would get to Shepherd Market by Shanks's pony – if the damned beast could be trusted not to collapse on the way. With the prospect of swings and roundabouts at the end of the journey, it surely wouldn't fail him.

He hadn't had an adventure in mind when he'd entered the restaurant deliberately late, already slightly sozzled. It was that boring banker bugger's talk about churches and iron and cemeteries that had turned his thoughts towards the occupation that had inspired him and his firstborn to ever greater manoeuvres during their best years. He'd excused the captain from the table and had phoned his requirements to his regular supplier : a buxom brunette, he'd said, would do very nicely, so long as she had enough breath in her well-covered lungs to last the course. Cuthbert had just the girl for him. Her working name was Francesca, but she was used to being called Frankie, because most of her customers were too bloody pig-ignorant to cope with a foreign handle.

He'd had the shudders all evening, thanks to Mr Harker. He'd seen the trees, and heard Skin-and-Bone. He'd felt, even while he was drinking cognac, that swift, icy clutch. Had he been capable of doing so, he might have screamed.

The medieval tomb could do without its knight for a while, although he was expected to take his place there. He needed something other than the comfort of a clammy hand pressed affectionately in his; he needed to be reminded that he wasn't in his second childhood. The frenzy that had long gone from his relationship with Mrs Hunter was exactly what he needed tonight.

'What I need is frenzy. It's frenzy I want.'

Victor Harker was relieved to be alone at last in his hotel room. He had returned the captain's kindness — if that was the word — handsomely; he'd given him — no doubt of it — the finest meal it was possible to buy. He had discharged his duty. He was free now to forget the old fraud.

For a fraud the captain certainly was. Over cognac, he had begun to declaim, nothing less, the Kitchener bilge about the glory of one's country and the honour of one's regiment, and more of that ancient, sickening palaver. Private Harker had listened politely, hoping that the flow would cease. He'd interrupted the torrent — for that's what it had threatened to become: an unstoppable torrent — by saying: 'I can't stomach any more of this, Captain.

I saw my friend George Popplewell blown to pieces in front of me. I saw what remained of his face. I saw his brains spilling out. They were good brains. They were wasted.'

It was then that the captain had had another of his sudden spasms.

'You must have seen hundreds of men die like that, Captain. I saw others killed, many of them, but only George comes to haunt me. You must have become hardened, to have pursued your military career with such success.'

The captain had merely stared.

'I would have fought in the last war, had my services been required. They weren't. I was told to keep up morale at home. I did. I helped put out a few fires. The idea of fighting Hitler made sense to me, Captain, but I didn't know then, and I don't know now, what or why I was fighting in France.'

The captain had continued to stare.

'Do *you* know? Can *you* tell me?'

For answer Victor Harker had received a request for a third tot of Boney's brew, if it was agreeable. The stuff did Hal's constitution a power of good.

He had watched the captain polish off a bowl of Turkish delight with shaking hands.

'I told you Hal had a sweet tooth, didn't I?'

'Lovely big titties. Lovely big titties.'
  'I've had very few complaints about them.'
  'Lovely veins. Lovely flesh.'
  'Try not to bite so hard. There's a love.'
  'Life. Life.'
  'Do what?'

'Life!'

'That's right, old-timer. That's right.'

'Lovely, lovely life.'

'As you say.'

'Lovely nipples. Lovely brown berries.'

'Nobody's ever called them berries before.'

'He wouldn't. He couldn't.'

'He? Who's he?'

'Him, of course. What if he's...? What if...?'

'What do you mean — "what if"? Don't glare at me like that, old-timer.'

'Horace hasn't been with you, has he? Not Horace?'

'He may have. I may have met dozens of Horaces. Who's Horace?'

'I saw him on my way here. He was asleep in a doorway. He was smelling to high heaven as usual.'

'He doesn't sound like my kind of gentleman. I don't cater to the trash off the streets. You can put your mind at rest, old-timer — he hasn't so much as looked at Frankie.'

'You are Francesca. You are my lovely Francesca.'

'That's me.'

'A lovely girl with lovely eyes and lovely lips.'

'That's right. I'm a lovely girl, let's agree. Now, why don't we both concentrate for a while?'

'Two lots of lovely lips.'

'That's right. And they're just for you. But go easy.'

'Action stations, Hal.'

'Your name's — easy, I said — Hal, is it?'

'Sometimes.'

'Do what?'

'I'm Hal when it suits me.'

'Whatever you say.'

'This is better than being medieval.'

'Mediwhat?'

'Frenzy is. Lovely, lovely frenzy. Frenzy's better than holding hands on a tomb.'

'I should hope so. Don't be morbid.'

'Hal's never morbid. Against his principles. Never.'

'I think you should save your breath for what you're doing.'

'You leave the thinking to me.'

'It was only a suggestion.'

'I'm quite a performer, aren't I?'

'That's right.'

'There's still life in me.'

'There is, old-timer. There is.'

'You should have seen me once. You should have seen me in the days when the Charleston was the rage. The energy I had!'

'You really ought to save your breath.'

'Francesca. Francesca.'

'Hal. You did say Hal, didn't you?'

'I believe so. Hal's who I am.'

'You're a funny old-timer. Easy!'

'Hal, yes. Yes, Hal. I'm Hal.'

'Easy. Easy.'

'Lovely, lovely Francesca.'

'Don't yawn in my face! You're not going to drop off, are you?'

'No. No, no. I might see trees.'

'Trees?'

'And hear them, too. Hear them rattling.'

'That's right.'

'They didn't always make a noise.'

'Concentrate.'

'It's only since him. It's only since Skin-and-Bone.'

'Concentrate.'

'There were no flowers. I looked around for them, but there weren't any. Of course there weren't.'

'Too much talking and see what happens. Lie back, old-timer. Frankie — sorry, Francesca — will make him grow again. You just let Francesca do the work. That's more like it. He's perking up already. Don't worry. A lot of gentlemen your age run out of steam. This is nice, isn't it? Look, he's kicking again. No, no — lie back. You're not the first to cry, old-timer. Hal. If I had a penny for every gentleman that cried, I'd be the wealthiest girl in London. No, no — you let Francesca do the work. She'll do some riding in a minute when she's sure he's ready. She'll put a smile on Hal's face. Relax, relax. That's right. There we are. Nice and snug, aren't we? Let Francesca do the moving. Isn't that nice? Isn't that nice, eh?'

'If I had to die, I'd like it to be now.'

'Don't be so morbid.'

'If I have to die, let it be on active duty.'

'Francesca wouldn't care for that, old-timer.'

'Hal would.'

'There! You made it.'

'Oh. Lovely, lovely. Oh.'

'Wasn't that nice?'

'Hal wants more. They used to pay Hal for more. Hal wants to do the riding.'

'Not tonight. You'll have to make another appointment. My maid will fix a date. Cuth's got me heavily booked till morning.'

'Hal wants more frenzy.'

'Some other time. Be a good boy and go and wash. That's an order, old-timer. Cuth can turn very nasty when he wants to. Francesca wouldn't want you to come to any harm.'

'Poor old Hal. My poor old Hal.'

'Dearest cagy, I never thought I should have to tell *you* to be practical. It's typical of you to want to raise my hopes, but I shan't ever visit Africa, and you know it. The garden's about as far as my strength will take me.'

What a terrible irony it was that she, his 'catch', his girl, should have died before him. For years he had worried that she might be widowed young: 'You'll promise me, won't you, Stella, that you'll marry again?' He had constantly imagined her left alone, in their rambling house, pining for the man she had freed from dustiness. 'I won't promise any such thing,' she'd snapped. 'There are plenty of fish in the sea, I know, but most of them deserve to stay there.'

Victor Harker drew a pillow into his arms and clutched it tightly.

Dressed as Captain Standish once more, the man for whom the trees were now in a commotion left Francesca's place of business and descended the stairs to the street. He passed a man in a burnous going up, but he did not notice him.

Blackness overcame him at Hyde Park Corner and he was suddenly no one. His body fell to the ground as a dead body falls.

Seven

He was not with Mrs Hunter. He was not in Julian's room. He was not in the Mission.

He was in a bed, surrounded by screens. He was wearing ragged pyjamas that stank of bleach.

'I'm not in a hospital, am I?'

A nurse appeared as he spoke. He could tell she was a nurse because she looked at him with bewildered sympathy. He saw her expression before he saw her uniform.

'That's precisely where you are.'

She placed a thermometer under his tongue and checked his pulse.

'Who's a lucky man?'

She removed the thermometer and examined it.

'Why am I?'

'I beg your pardon?'

'Why am I lucky?'

'Because you are.'

She smiled at something above his head and left. He stared after her.

'I hate hospitals. I hate hospitals.'

He glimpsed the uniform through tears. He wiped his eyes and became aware that the woman inside it was black.

'Good morning.'

'It's morning, is it?'

'Turned six.'

'It could be any time in here.'

'I have some questions to ask you.'

'What questions?'

'I have to get your record straight. First of all, what's your name?'

'Name?'

'Everyone has a name.'

'It depends on the clothes I was wearing.'

The nurse laughed.

'I'm serious. Was I wearing corduroy?'

'No.'

'Was I dressed for the dosshouse?'

'Certainly not.'

'My teeth will tell me who I am. Where are they?'

'They're with your things. I'll see that you get them back.'

'Did I pass out?'

'You collapsed. In the street.'

'Did I have a suit on? A kind of tropical suit, made of linen?'

'Yes.'

'Then I am Captain Harold Standish.'

The nurse wrote the name on an official form.

'And your address?'

'Address?'

'Everyone has a home.'

'There you are wrong, my beauty. There you are very wrong. Should you consult the worthy Sergeant Marybeth, you will be informed to the contrary.'

'I'm sure *you* have an address. I can't imagine *you* not having one.'

'Don't be too sure.'

'You're enjoying your little game, aren't you?'

'Perhaps.'

'I can see you are. Your address, please.'

'I wanted to keep it a secret. The world is full of snoopers.' He whispered: 'It's 221b Baker Street, London, West One.'

'Are you above a shop?'

'Not that I know of.'

'Baker Street has some beautiful shops. I bought a leather coat in a sale there once.'

'When I last looked, I wasn't above a shop.'

'Do you have a religion?'

'Not to my knowledge.'

'I'll put you down as Church of England.'

'Put down whatever you wish. A holy Roman. A primitive Methodist. A wandering Jew.'

He was in the field. The shapes of men were ahead of him. In the distance, the trees were rattling.

He was paralysed, as always. The sky turned red, and so did the earth. When he tried to scream, strange words leapt from him: Etaples, Amiens, Neuve Chapelle, Rheims, Rouen. 'Montreuil' was on his lips when he awoke.

The screens had been taken away. He was one among many in a long ward. In the bed to his right, he noticed with horror, was a youth with the wasted looks of Skin-and-Bone. He turned from the awful spectacle. The man to his left was comfortingly bald and fat.

He was still without the captain's teeth.

He began to blubber as soon as the test was over.

'What did you do that for? Why did you do that to me?'

'To find out if you have an ulcer,' the doctor replied. 'You haven't.'

'I nearly choked to – ' He could not say the word. 'I nearly choked.'

'You'll survive.'

'I couldn't breathe.'

'We're going to look after you for a few days. You're slightly anaemic. We'll put some fresh blood in you.'

'Whose?'

'Someone's.'

'Tell me whose.'

'Mr Jones's. Or then again, Mr Smith's.'

'Bring me the captain's pearlies. Let me be Hal.'

'The war will end when the Golden Virgin falls,' he said to the black nurse as she tucked him in.

'The war's been over a long time, Captain. It ended five years before I was born.'

'Why did I say that?'

'Search me.'

'I couldn't help myself. The words just came into my head. Who is the Golden Virgin?'

'I haven't a clue.'

'I think I'm losing control. I think I'm breaking up,' he sobbed.

'You're tired, that's all. You need to rest. The doctor told me you've been a naughty boy lately. He said you've been doing things you shouldn't. A good rest is what you need.'

'I don't want to dream. I have to stay awake. I don't want to find myself.'

'You're talking in riddles because you're tired and ill.'

'I'm frightened. I'm scared.'

'You've nothing to be afraid of.'

'I'm terrified, I tell you.'

'Drink this hot milk.'

He did as she instructed, and was soon asleep.

Despite his efforts to escape, the field eventually claimed him. Its red grass spoke to him. It whispered : 'You're too young to die. You're too young to die.'

'Yes,' he said. 'I am.'

'A handsome blighter like you.'

'A handsome blighter like me.'

He was no longer paralysed. His young limbs moved swiftly, surely. They took him into the trees, and beyond the trees into towns with foreign names. They took him into the warm night, with its insect noises and its tiny, watchful, suddenly scampering animals. They took him away from death. They took him away from guns and wounds and howitzers.

Eric Talbot's blood coursed in his young veins.

He it was who found King Solomon's mines; he it was who peered down a valley into the Lost World.

He was called in to tea.

He would be brave one day. He would be fearless. He would not be like Gerald Talbot, a dull commercial traveller who wrote poetry in his spare time. He would be a man of action.

'Your father is dead, Eric. I've made cucumber sandwiches. He did away with himself; he did himself in. And your favourite chocolate cake. In Hull, of all places. There's jelly, too. You and I will have to make a go of things. Sit straight, dear – sit straight. Between us, we'll make a life for you. I bought cream as a special treat. In Hull, my dear, in a common lodgings. Be mother, Eric – pour for both of us. He left a note. There was no mention of me. Or you. It was addressed to Shelley. What a coward, Eric. What a perfectly disgusting coward.'

Exhausted by dreams, he watched as the gift from Mr Jones or Mr Smith dripped into his strapped-up arm.

'The stuff of life.'

Here was the stuff that he had feared shedding; here was the stuff that had made the earth change colour. Here was the stuff – although it was Mr Jones's, or then again, Mr Smith's – that had kept a nameless man alive for sixty-odd years.

They had been very odd years.

To be laughing and crying, to be shrieking and bawling, is to be hysterical, he told Eric Talbot.

Visitors arrived, bearing flowers.

He heard the youth in the next bed say, 'I can't bear it, Auntie Iris. I can't take it. I was doing all right until they brought him in. I was doing fine. It's not just that he's old, though that's bad enough. He talks in his sleep, and he cries. He talks filth, Auntie – real filth. If it isn't filth, it's to do with death. He must have been a soldier, I think – and not a very brave one either. He woke me early this morning with his screaming. He was shouting something about guns and gas and bombs. He's mad, Auntie. It's not my imagination – he's out of his mind. He upsets me. I don't want to end up like him. I wouldn't want to end up like him. Ask them to move me to another ward. Please ask them, Auntie Iris.'

'Captain Standish? Hal?'

It was not Auntie Iris who was looking down at him.

'You remember me, surely? Victor Harker. Victor.'

'Oh, yes. The banker. How did you find me?'

'You'd written my name, and the phone number of my hotel, on a piece of paper. It was in your jacket when you had the accident. Someone from the hospital rang me.'

'So we meet again.'

'Yes. How are you?'

'I ought to say I'm not myself, but that would be a lie.'

'You're very pale.'

'That's why this bag's feeding me.'

'I hope there's nothing seriously wrong with you.'

'Do you really? Do you really give a damn?'

'I hate to see anyone suffer.'

'Even me?'

'Even you.'

'Sit down. Don't hover. Keep me company.'

'I brought you some grapes. I couldn't think of anything else to bring.'

'Thank you. I hate hospitals.'

'So do I.'

'I last saw the inside of one half a century ago. It was in the country. I spent months in the dump. I ran away again and became an inventor.'

'Again?'

'Listen to me carefully. "The war will end when the Golden Virgin falls." Am I making sense?'

'Yes.'

'Then tell me what I'm saying.'

'You must have been in France.'

'I was.'

'You must have been in France when I was there.'

'I was.'

'You must have fought on the Somme.'

'I didn't. I ran away. I deserted.'

'How could you have done? It was impossible, virtually impossible, to escape.'

'I managed it. I slept in cowsheds by day and ran by night. A farmer's wife took care of me for a time. I screwed her senseless. I was a handsome blighter.'

'But, Hal – '

'I'm Eric. Private Eric Talbot. No one else. Tell me about the Golden Virgin.'

'It was a statue on a cathedral.'

'You and your churches.'

'Yes. On a cathedral, if I remember correctly, in a town called Albert – the boys always said the name in an English way. The statue was on the tower, right at the top. It was of the Virgin Mary holding the infant Jesus. A German shell struck the tower and the statue was almost broken off. It was leaning over the square below when I first saw it.'

'And when I did, too.'

'It was said that the war would end on the day it finally fell off.' Victor Harker paused. 'I'm mystified.'

'It's a simple story. I wanted to live, so I ran away.'

'And the captain?'

'In the hospital's possession, teeth and all.' He added, in Julian's voice: 'I believe you saw me at Marble Arch.'

'It *was* you.'

'It was Julian, my last born. My unholy trinity consisted of Hal, whose company you so much enjoyed – ' he winked ' – and a gentleman of the road called Tommy, and Julian Borrow, whose poetry I could churn out at will. The three of them kept boredom and Eric Talbot at bay for many, many years.'

'Incredible.'

'I must be a genius of sorts, I agree. I seem to recall that Eric was a brilliant boy, but it's a hazy memory. I lost my childhood somewhere between France and England. I tried to recapture it in the loony bin, but it wouldn't come back. I ran away a second time. I arrived in London without my name. I was bored, bored. I became an inventor. Of people. Hal and his joystick were prominent features of the roaring 'twenties. I'm a shocking individual, aren't I?'

'I wouldn't say "shocking" – '

'Wouldn't you? What about "devilish"? "Brilliant"? No matter. The time has come to lock up the box of tricks for ever. The show's over. I can be

weary now. For a little, little while I can be the man
I lost.'

'Would you express my sincere gratitude to Mr
Jones and Mr Smith?' he said to the nurse who un-
strapped his arm. 'They've made me feel like a new
man.'

Shortly after midnight he got out of bed and
walked shakily to the end of the ward. 'I am going
to the lavatory,' he explained to the nurse on duty.
'I'll be back in a moment.'

The corridors were all but deserted. The hospital
staff, he said to himself, are engaged in the business
of healing — they've done with me, and I've done
with them.

'Where are you going?' a porter asked him.

'Just taking a constitutional,' he replied.

He raced past the reception desk. Voices called
after him.

He stopped, panting, in a side-street. He breathed
in the warm night air. Ragged pyjamas stinking of
bleach were the ideal outfit for tropical weather.

'To the Thames, Eric Talbot. To the Thames.'

He set off purposefully towards the river. He was
ready to make his greatest escape, to stage his positively final disappearance. Death, which he had
feared in France, was welcoming him, and he was
happy to be free at last to accept the invitation.

'No shudders. No spasms.'

People stared at the strange old man who walked
with such determination. Some of them laughed at
him. London was filled with lunatics.

He noticed that his feet were bleeding when he

reached the river. He offered his apologies to Mr Smith and Mr Jones.

Eric Talbot stood on the bridge and looked down at the water. 'It's nearly dried up,' he said. 'Still, I expect there will be enough of the stuff to cover me.'

He climbed on to the parapet and jumped. He saw the Golden Virgin break loose and knew that the war was over.

Eight

The train moved slowly out of the station. Victor Harker smiled a natural smile. The prison would never claim him again.

He would savour each part of the journey. He was going home. He was returning to those emblems of Stella's absence which would now remind him of her loving presence. Tonight he would be surrounded once more by their shared treasures – the books, the music, the photographs; the pots, the pans.

When he had first arrived in Newcastle, what a shadow of a man he'd been. He had had no friends and no relatives, for Lizzie had emigrated to Australia with her husband and had sent him no address. His possessions had fitted easily into a small suitcase.

Dusty Victor Harker had worked and worked in the dirty Northern city. Each evening, after a long day's slaving at the bank, he had studied hard at his evening class, and then – in his dingy room – he had burned the midnight oil while his fellow lodgers slept. He was seldom discouraged. His father's whine and the hare's leap were the only spurs he'd needed.

And then, when he had achieved his ambition, and the dust had looked like settling on him for the remainder of his life, he had met Miss Stella Palmer, the daughter of Mr Oswald Palmer, his bank's most favoured client.

'My father disapproves of you. Let him live with his disapproval.'

He smiled again, remembering her. He had wept for her in the hotel – for the slow and steady manner of her dying; for the pain she'd borne. Yet the tears which had eased his heart had sprung from some other source – from the remembrance of her honesty, her visible lack of deception. Only honesty, he thought, can send dust scattering and unlock cages.

Still smiling, he fell asleep.

He was on a route march. He was breaking-in his soft feet and his new boots.

He was scooping up stew from a zinc bath in which the regiment's tea had been brewed earlier that day.

He was on a boat bound for France, where the war was being fought and women knew a thing or two.

He was drinking rum before the battle, to put some spark in him.

He was laughing – helplessly, crazily – at the sight he had spent months waiting for; the inside of his friend George Popplewell's head.

'Calm yourself.'

He was returning to sanity, to the rambling house – with its view over the moor – that contained the evidence of love.

He remembered, with dismay, that he had given his address to Eric Talbot.

'Oh, Stella. How could I have been such a fool?
Oh, my darling, darling Stella.'

Distressed, he stared out at the parched earth
speeding past.

He smiled at what he saw.

'Look, my darling. Cheetahs.'

Nine

Eric Talbot was identified as Captain Harold Standish by a disconsolate Mrs Hunter. How little, she thought, I knew him – my happy, naughty old boy.

'I never had an inkling,' she told the coroner, 'that suicide was on his mind. I still can't believe he's done it. His eyes had their usual sparkle the last time we said goodbye.'

Prayers were said at the Mission for the soul of Tommy, who had disappeared, as many of Sergeant Marybeth's strays had done.

How could people vanish so? It was a constant mystery. It was as if they dug holes in the earth and tunnelled themselves out of sight.

'Perhaps I'm being precipitous. Perhaps he's still alive. Perhaps he'll pop up again, as the groundhogs do in Manitoba.'

'He was decent,' said Horace. 'He was the most decent bloke I ever see.'

'Dear God,' the sergeant whispered to her Maker, 'stop my wicked thoughts. Stop me wishing that this one of all my strays had vanished instead.'

Julian Borrow's room was cleared of its junk and rented to a student from Palestine. The poet's wallpaper was painted over. Posters expressive of a glorious future replaced the messages of rejection and regret.

The ashes of Victor Harker were scattered, like Stella's, among squalling seabirds.

FOR THE BEST IN PAPERBACKS, LOOK FOR THE 🐧

In every corner of the world, on every subject under the sun, Penguin represents quality and variety – the very best in publishing today.

For complete information about books available from Penguin – including Pelicans, Puffins, Peregrines and Penguin Classics – and how to order them, write to us at the appropriate address below. Please note that for copyright reasons the selection of books varies from country to country.

In the United Kingdom: For a complete list of books available from Penguin in the U.K., please write to *Dept E.P., Penguin Books Ltd, Harmondsworth, Middlesex, UB7 0DA*

In the United States: For a complete list of books available from Penguin in the U.S., please write to *Dept BA, Penguin, 299 Murray Hill Parkway, East Rutherford, New Jersey 07073*

In Canada: For a complete list of books available from Penguin in Canada, please write to *Penguin Books Canada Ltd, 2801 John Street, Markham, Ontario L3R 1B4*

In Australia: For a complete list of books available from Penguin in Australia, please write to the *Marketing Department, Penguin Books Australia Ltd, P.O. Box 257, Ringwood, Victoria 3134*

In New Zealand: For a complete list of books available from Penguin in New Zealand, please write to the *Marketing Department, Penguin Books (NZ) Ltd, Private Bag, Takapuna, Auckland 9*

In India: For a complete list of books available from Penguin, please write to *Penguin Overseas Ltd, 706 Eros Apartments, 56 Nehru Place, New Delhi, 110019*

In Holland: For a complete list of books available from Penguin in Holland, please write to *Penguin Books Nederland B.V., Postbus 195, NL–1380AD Weesp, Netherlands*

In Germany: For a complete list of books available from Penguin, please write to *Penguin Books Ltd, Friedrichstrasse 10 – 12, D–6000 Frankfurt Main 1, Federal Republic of Germany*

In Spain: For a complete list of books available from Penguin in Spain, please write to *Longman Penguin España, Calle San Nicolas 15, E–28013 Madrid, Spain*

THE HEART IS A LONELY HUNTER
Carson McCullers

The story of a group of people in the American south which explores their individual response to the gentle, sympathetic appeal of a deaf-mute – and their common factor, loneliness.

FIRE ON THE MOUNTAIN
Anita Desai

The portrait of a strange relationship between two solitary people, and a wonderfully observed picture of life in India by one of her foremost living writers.

'Beautifully accomplished . . . I admired it unreservedly' – Susan Hill

A CONFEDERACY OF DUNCES
John Kennedy Toole

'I succumbed, stunned and seduced, page after page . . . It is a masterwork of comedy', said *The New York Times* of this Pulitzer prize-winning novel. Outrageous, grotesque, superbly written, its Falstaffian hero is Ignatius J. Reilly, a self-proclaimed genius in a world of dunces.

THE LOVE DEPARTMENT
William Trevor

'A fantasy which proliferates entertainingly from a germ of reality – the reality of boredom felt by comfortably-off suburban wives . . . Mr Trevor's scenes range from the near-realistic to the completely fantastic, while his tone blends the humorous, the satirical, and the sympathetic with a touch of the sinister' – *Listener*

THE YAWNING HEIGHTS
Alexander Zinoviev

Clive James has called this larger than life satire on contemporary Russian society 'a work vital to the continuity of civilization'.

A selection

THE BLOODY CHAMBER
Angela Carter

In these reworkings of classic fairy tales Angela Carter
'combines exquisite craft with an apparently boundless imaginative
reach' – Ian McEwan

THE TWYBORN AFFAIR
Patrick White

As his androgynous hero, Eudoxia/Eddie/Eadith Twyborn, searches
for self-affirmation and for love in its many forms, the author of
Voss takes us on a tremendous journey into the ambiguous landscapes,
sexual, psychological and spiritual, of the human condition.

BLACK TICKETS
Jayne Anne Phillips

'Jayne Anne Phillips has blasted the American short story out of
suburbia and restored it to its former glory' – Nadine Gordimer

SOLARIS/THE CHAIN OF CHANCE/
A PERFECT VACUUM
Stanislaw Lem

An omnibus edition including *Solaris*, Lem's most celebrated science
fiction novel which has appeared in over twenty languages.

'His imagination is so powerful and pure that no matter what world he
creates it is immediately convincing . . . A virtuoso storyteller, a major
writer and one of the deep spirits of our age' – *The New York Times*

LAMB
Bernard Mac Laverty

This story of a priest and a boy from the Dublin slums who attempt to
live by an ideal of love becomes an image of piercing simplicity.
Bernard Mac Laverty's brilliant first novel is the work of 'a born writer
with a manifest destiny' – *Sunday Times*

A Choice of Penguin Fiction

THE HEAT OF THE DAY
Elizabeth Bowen

Wartime London: and Stella's lover, Robert, is suspected of selling information to the enemy. Harrison, shadowing Robert, is nonetheless prepared to bargain, and the price is Stella.

Elizabeth Bowen writes of three people, estranged from the past and reluctant to trust in the future, with the psychological insight and delicate restraint that have earned her a position among the most distinguished novelists of the century.

A MONTH IN THE COUNTRY
J. L. Carr
Winner of the *Guardian* Fiction Prize

In the summer of 1920 two men meet in the quiet English countryside. One is a war survivor, living in the church, intent upon uncovering and restoring a historical wall-painting. The other, too, is a war survivor, camping in the next field in search of a lost grave. And out of their physical meeting comes a deeper communion, with the landscape, with history, and a catching up of the old primeval rhythms of life – past and present – so cruelly disorientated by the Great War.

A PAINTED DEVIL
Rachel Billington

In this stark, chilling book, Rachel Billington explores the complexities of creative egotism and its power first to enchant its victims, and then to destroy them.

Edward is a painter. With the selfishness of a dedicated artist, he feeds upon the sufferings of others, unaware of the destruction and despair that crashes around him.

And Florence in winter provides a setting for this story of two men and one woman, bound together in a strange love affair.

DOCTOR FISCHER OF GENEVA OR THE BOMB PARTY

Graham Greene

Doctor Fischer despises the human race. When the notorious toothpaste millionaire decides to hold his own deadly version of the Book of Revelations, Greene opens up a powerful vision of the limitless greed of the rich: black comedy and painful satire combine in a totally compelling novel.

'Manages to say more about love, hate, happiness, grief, immortality, greed and the disgustingly rich that most contemporary English novels three times in length' – *The Times*

YOUR LOVER JUST CALLED

Stories of Joan and Richard Maple

John Updike

Joan and Richard Maple confess infidelities; join a Boston civil rights march; take a trip to the in-laws, to the beach, to Rome; and after twenty years – a million mundane moments shared – attempt to explain to their four children why they have decided to separate.

With astonishing power and tenderness, John Updike traces the story of their marriage: a marriage that begins with love and ends, irretrievably, with love.

DESPAIR

Vladimir Nabokov

Hermann and his Russian wife, Lydia, are *la crème de la crème* of the middle class – or so it would seem. On a business trip to Prague, Hermann stumbles across a man he believes to be his double and starts plotting to turn the meeting to his advantage.

'A beautiful mystery plot, not to be revealed. It is enough to say that this book . . . again reveals Nabokov as the last European' – *Newsweek*

NUNS AND SOLDIERS
Iris Murdoch

Gertrude has lost her husband and Anne, an ex-nun, her
God. They plan to live together and do good works. Polish exile and
imaginary soldier, the 'Count' watches over Gertrude with
loving patience. An accomplished scrounger and failed painter, Tim
is a different sort of soldier. He plans, with his eccentric
mistress Daisy, to live off rich friends.

A fine and riveting novel from Iris Murdoch and, as Martin Amis said
in the *Observer*, 'you certainly don't want it to end'.

THE SPINOZA OF MARKET STREET
Isaac Bashevis Singer

'Mr Singer is one of those rare writers – Hans Andersen is another –
whose original work reads like a fable. These phantasmagoric
tales of Polish Jewry, most of which are historical in their setting, are
the nearest thing in literature to the paintings of Bosch.
Their humour and their passion is that of a whole culture' – *Sunday
Telegraph*

THE GREAT AMERICAN NOVEL
Philip Roth

'A comic extravaganza – a sprawling burlesque which rambles
over the myths, the prejudices, the history and the literature of
America' – *The Times Literary Supplement*

'His subject is as American as apple crumble, it is baseball, and while
the extravagance and comedy and grotesquerie of the treatment
keep the reader's head delightedly spinning, it has deliberately serious
implications for the American way of life' – *Financial Times*

Autobiographies from writers in Penguins

ABOUT TIME

Penelope Mortimer

Winner of the Whitbread Award

Her ironic and delightful autobiography of girlhood between the wars. After leaving her fifth school, Penelope Mortimer was sent to train as a secretary, but soon moved on, via London University and Bloomsbury, to marriage and the birth of her first daughter in Hitler's Vienna. On the outbreak of war, she celebrated her twenty-first birthday in the Café de Paris – 'we drank champagne to the present and future, but not to the past, that I have tried to celebrate here'.

'It goes down not so much like a madeleine as like a lemon water-ice on a hot day, sharp and gritty as well as smooth and sweet... leaving a taste for more' – *Listener*

SMILE PLEASE

An unfinished autobiography

Jean Rhys

'She was indeed an extraordinary writer and had a completely original voice' – *Financial Times*

Jean Rhys's strange and haunting novels distill the alienation and despair of women who have – somehow – slipped a little. Here, from the early days on Dominica, to gin-and-bedsitter life in England, to Paris with her first husband, she gives us a rich, funny as well as moving autobiography of her early life.

MEMORIES OF A CATHOLIC GIRLHOOD

Mary McCarthy

'There is an element of *tour de force* in this brilliant book' – *Observer*

Blending memories and family myths, Mary McCarthy takes us back to the twenties, when she was orphaned into a world of relations as colourful, potent and mysterious as the Catholic religion. From her black veiled Jewish grandmother to her wicked Uncle Myers who beat her for the good of her soul, here are the people who inspired her devastating sense of the sublime and ridiculous, and her witty, novelist's imagination.